Chasing Spirit

ELEMENTUM MYTH

BOOK 1

DESI LIN

LITERARY SERVICES

Cover Design Copyright © 2023 L&L Literary Services, LLC

Book Design Copyright © 2023 L&L Literary Services, LLC

www.llliteraryservices.com

Copy Editing by L&L Literary Services, LLC

Printed in the United States of America.

ISBN: 978-1-953437-89-1

First Printing, 2023

ACKNOWLEDGMENTS

This story is special. All stories are, of course, but this one is especially close to my heart. This is the story that spurred me to publish. When this story started, it was a fluffy piece of fun for me and a few others, then it was a fluffy piece of fun shared with a few more people.

From the response I got then, I started to believe that I might have something to share with the world. This story has gone through several revisions since those early days, especially after Sera burst onto the scene. I could never have done it alone. So many people helped this book come into your hands.

K. Swanson – my incredible partner in crime (I mean writing. Yeah. Writing.) for keeping me on track (and occasionally getting me off track). For maintaining my sanity through all the nuttiness of my life. For being the incredible support I need.

Lyn – who helps me make sure I put my best story forward. Who never fails to answer my three thousand questions.

My writing group – for about three million things. Seriously, you are all awesome, and I love you.

Amanda – you were there at the beginning of this journey. Without you, this world may not exist at all. You finally got Ash's story.

My family – My biggest and most vocal supporters. You put up with so much from me and everything I've taken on. Thank you.

For Amanda, who waited so patiently for Ash's story

GLOSSARY

The Elementum are a society living within our own. They are as old as we are and, as such, developed in ways unique to them. Here you will find a reference for the terms used throughout this story.

Ventus – Person with control of air element

Ignis – Person with control of fire element

Terra – Person with control of earth element

Aqua – Person with control of water element

Genus – Group of Elementum whose abilities are strongest together. One element per Genus is the norm.

Iunctura – Joining of Elementum abilities into a Genus

Foederis – when an Iunctura is broken

Furcifer – an Elementum criminal

Sapientes/Sage – Elder Elementum who serve as leaders and advisors

Concilium Maximus – Grand Council. One Sapientes from each Elementum sits on this Concilium. These are the overall leaders of the Elementum.

Tabularium – the Elementum library and archives. One archive is located in each major metropolitan area that is home to Elementum.

Ad Aetatum – Coming of Age for an Elementum child. Takes place at eighteen. This is the first time an Iunctura can occur. This is a big deal in the Elementum world.

Lex – Elementum Police

Scholae – Headmaster of the Illustratio Academy.

Quintus – Slang term for the fifth Elementum, supposedly just a myth.

Menda – Person born to Elementum parents without any abilities.

Normal.

It's such an everyday word. A word that people don't really think about often. We don't bother to define it, question it, or explain it. It is what it is, until it isn't, then it gets redefined in the mind. We are adaptable, us humans. We've proven it time and again, shifting our cultures and beliefs, and religions and societies. Normal is what we choose to make it.

CHAPTER ONE

RAEGAN

Darkness shrouded the parking lot as we left the movie theater. Back home, all the parking lots were well-lit, but in Marysville, it seemed people forgot that lights were a good thing when movies didn't let out until after midnight.

A breeze ruffled my pin-straight, white hair.

With a shiver, I wrapped my arms around my middle and hunched my shoulders. Even after nearly a year here, I still wasn't used to how cold it was, even in June. Next time we'd be out this late, I'd remember to wear more than just jeans and a long-sleeved T-shirt.

The weight of a long, black trench coat settled on

my shoulders. Shooting Pierson a grateful look, I snuggled into the warmth.

"I told you to grab a jacket, but no, it would ruin the look," Pierson teased as we made our way to the back of the lot, where we'd parked.

I shot him a mock glare.

At the deep chuckle on my other side, I turned my glare on Devin, too.

"Oh, come on Pier, don't you know by now? Fashion before function." Devin reached over and mussed my hair.

Stupid brother. I smacked at his hand, which did exactly diddly squat, so instead, I reached out and shoved him.

Devin stumbled back a step, and just as he was moving in to retaliate, a blond blur threw itself at him.

"Devin! Hi!" The high-pitched, breathless voice came out of a tiny, blond girl I vaguely recognized from school, Cherry or Sherri or Cary... Something like that, anyway.

The girl wrapped herself around Devin, pressing so tight against him I was sure they could hold a piece of paper securely between their bodies.

With a sigh, I rolled my eyes in Pierson's direction. This happened every damn time we went somewhere with Devin, sometimes two or three different times.

What was it about my brother that had girls throwing themselves at him? Was it the black hair and deep brown eyes? His tall, lanky build? The colorful array of tattoos? Or his *don't-give-a-shit* attitude?

Honestly, just looking at us, no one would guess we were related. With my own naturally white hair and pale gray eyes, short stature, soft curves, and nearly tattoo-free skin, I was the exact opposite of Devin.

In the past, our differences earned us the nicknames Yin and Yang. It used to bother me all the time, but lately, I missed it. With Devin and me being four years apart and moving here at the start of my senior year of high school, we didn't have the same circle of friends. Not like back home, where we'd known most of the people in our city for nearly our whole lives. I had to admit, though, I'd never been as close to anyone back home as I was to Pierson.

We met when he'd cut through our yard the day we moved in. When I yelled at him, he'd rolled his eyes and said he always cut through there and wasn't about to change that. Turned out Pierson lived in the

3

house behind ours. He'd been my best friend ever since.

A high-pitched giggle cut through my thoughts.

Mildly annoyed by Cherry-Sherri-Cary's blatant flirting, I turned to Pierson again, only to find him watching Devin and the blond.

He swallowed hard and turned away.

I grabbed his hand, squeezed, then bumped him with my shoulder. "So, are you looking forward to college in the fall?"

My attempt to distract him didn't work, because Pierson only shrugged and kept his gaze on the pavement. I hated that I couldn't say anything, couldn't talk about the pink elephant. It killed me to see him so uncomfortable. I couldn't push things, though, no matter how much I wanted to make it all better.

A hand landed on Pier's shoulder, and we both jumped before turning to find Devin behind us.

"Sorry about that. I had a hard time peeling Terri off me." Devin waggled his eyebrows at Pierson.

Pierson jerked out from under Devin's hand and stalked off toward the car.

With a shrug, Devin looked at me. "What'd I say?"

Heaven save me from clueless men.

Shaking my head, I jogged after my friend.

I closed the distance Pierson put between us. "Do you maybe have anything you want to talk about?"

Please say yes.

Pierson stopped, tipping his head back to stare up at the sky. He only did that when he was thinking.

Moving around to his front, I set my hands on his shoulders. He'd quit shaving since school ended, and the beginning of a small beard speckled across his square jawline.

Pierson lowered his blue gaze to meet my own. "No, Raegan. I'm fine. Really."

He smiled, trying to alleviate my concerns, I was sure, but I didn't miss the sadness and anxiety on his face. He had to work through this on his own, though. All I could do was make sure he knew I was here when he was ready.

I nodded, holding in my disappointment as I turned to continue toward the car. When Pier didn't move, I glanced back over my shoulder to find him waiting for Devin to catch up, so I went on ahead. I just wanted to get to the car.

The shadows seemed deeper in the back of the lot, somehow more ominous. I shivered again, and this time, the cold had nothing to do with it. The desire to be behind locked car doors made my feet move faster, but I wasn't the one with the keys.

One dim light stood nearby, and figuring it would be a good place to wait for the boys, I leaned against the pole. My eyes darted around, trying to find the source of my unease. All I found were the shadows and the boys, who'd stopped to talk.

My curiosity over what they might be discussing distracted me for a few moments until I swore I caught movement behind them. Before I could call out a warning, harsh hands grabbed me and pulled me into the shadows. Pain lanced through my arms at the crushing grip, and I fought to find my footing again, to pull away from my abductor.

"Devin! Pierson!" I screamed as my pulse raced and my heart pounded.

My frantic gaze scanned the lot for the boys, desperately hoping they were racing toward me. My hope shattered when I saw them fighting with five more guys, little more than shadows, preventing them from coming to my aid. Blood ran down Devin's face from a thin cut on his temple even as he landed a blow in one guy's gut. Another guy swept Pierson's legs from under him, and he hit the ground with a thud.

"Pierson! Devin!" I screamed again, fear heightening my panic as I was pulled along.

I fought harder against the grip on my arms, twisting and turning, hoping I could connect my foot to a shin or something and startle the abductor, maybe even get a look at them. My hair whipped around, striking my face as I struggled, blocking my vision.

A hard yank wrenched my shoulder, and I screamed in pain.

Finally getting my hair out of my face, I glanced at my abductor. In the darkness of the lot, I couldn't make out much detail. Fuck. Giving up, I sought out the boys again. Devin met my gaze and lunged toward me, only to be grabbed and thrown backward. Pierson, still on the ground, sat up and shook his head before trying to stand. As the distance grew between us, the shadows deepened. Soon, I'd be completely hidden from their sight.

"Get her in the damn car, you idiots!" a harsh, growling voice yelled.

Two guys came running over from the fight and snatched me up.

I screamed again, to no avail in the empty parking lot. When they shoved me into the trunk of a car, I tried to leap out, but they pushed me back in and slammed the trunk closed.

Tears streamed down my cheeks as I beat against the inside of the trunk. What did they want? Why me? I was nothing special! Just a normal, everyday girl. Hell, I even graduated high school a year later than everyone else because I was sick as hell when I was eight.

On the verge of hyperventilating, my breaths came faster. I punched against the trunk over and over, the dull thud of my fists echoing in my ears like a refrain. Sharp pain blazed across my knuckles, making me jerk my fist back. Swallowing the sob that tried to escape, I felt my hand, fingers encountering wetness that wasn't there before. I'd split my knuckles.

The reality of injuring myself had a sobering effect. Hysteria wouldn't help me out of this situation.

With a deep breath, I calmed my panicked brain. My first calm thought was for the boys, but I couldn't worry about them. Devin and Pierson were both tough and were likely seeking help. I needed to focus on the here and now. I wished I had a light.

Wait. My phone!

Patting my pockets turned up nothing, though. It must have dropped in the struggle.

Come on, Raegan, think!

What do you know about car trunks? Not much, unfortunately. Cars had never been high on the interest list for my family. My mind raced, hoping to find that one tidbit that would get me the hell out of there.

Wait! Hadn't Dad mentioned a safety feature about trunks when he and Mom were car shopping a couple years ago? What the heck was it? Trunk latch! That was it! A latch on the inside of trunks to open it from the inside. That was my ticket out.

My fingers raced along the trunk, my knuckles stinging as I searched. It took a few moments, but finally, I found the plastic pull tag. I wanted to yank on it right away and get the hell out of there, but common sense smacked down the instinct.

The car moved too fast to make bailing out now safe. If I did, I'd likely break a bone or worse. I needed to wait for the driver to idle at a stoplight. But knowing I had a way out and waiting to use it was almost worse than being trapped.

Finally, the car slowed to a stop. I yanked at the tag, shoved the trunk wide, and rolled out onto the asphalt just as the car drove away.

The rough road tore my clothes and skin. When I came to a stop, I looked up and found a pair of red converse inches from my head.

What new hell had I managed to find?

Swallowing, I raised my eyes, and my breath caught at the sheer amount of hotness in front of me. He was tall, with the hint of a tattoo peeking out from under his sleeve. The streetlight glinted off the golden highlights in his dark hair, and a crystal stud flashed in his ear.

"Well, I'm used to girls falling at my feet, but rolling is a new one," the guy quipped, grin wide and hazel eyes sparkling with mischief as he offered a hand.

My brain cells refused to fire, so I ended up just staring until he winked and waggled his hand in front of my face.

Heat rose in my cheeks as I took his hand and let him help me to my feet, the movement making me aware of the aches and pains in my body.

The hottie didn't miss my wince and ran an assessing gaze over me. "I'm guessing there's a story here?"

His gaze darted up to the quickly vanishing car before returning to me. He lifted my hand and kissed my split knuckles.

Was it okay to swoon right now? Because I did.

"I do think, though, that you ought to call the cops," he continued. "Do you have a cell phone?"

I blinked several times, my brain cells finally firing as I shook my head. What the hell was I going to do? I had no idea where I was and no way to call Devin, Pierson, or my folks.

"Come on. I don't live too far." He tipped his head, indicating the direction. "We can walk, and you can use my phone to call the cops. While we're there, you can get those cuts seen to. I'd let you use my phone here, but I left it at my house. My name's Ash, by the way."

CHAPTER TWO

ASH

I took in the mystery girl as I helped her to her feet.

She was a pretty thing with a light smattering of freckles across the bridge of her nose and hair so white I couldn't help but wonder how much bleach she used to get it that way.

The better question was, how the hell did she end up in the trunk of a car?

A sudden tug and snap in my gut, almost like a rubber band being pulled taut and released, had me sucking in a quick breath. The sensation was a familiar one, and also impossible. I already had a complete Genus. In Elementum society, we bonded with people from different elements that made us stronger as a whole, and all my spots were filled.

Mystery Girl swayed, and I moved my arm to wrap around her waist. "What's your name? Or I can just keep calling you Beautiful Mystery Girl."

Hopefully, the question would help her focus and calm. Poor thing shook in my arms.

After a few shaky breaths, she stuttered, "Rae… Raegan."

Half a smile crossed her face before her eyes darted behind her to where the car had been, and her brow creased.

I needed to get her out of here before the knuckleheads in the car realized she was gone.

"Come to my place." I released her and grabbed her hand again to lead her through the streets to the house I shared with my Genus.

She said nothing as we walked, and I appreciated the silence since it gave me time to process. I'd never heard of a Genus with five members, but the Iunctura was unmistakable. It happened when Elementum came into contact with those destined to join together in a Genus. Would the others feel it as well? Was our Genus breaking for some reason?

The empty, deserted road slowly gave way to houses. Raegan's hand trembled in mine despite the soft glow from the streetlights lining the sidewalk. When we passed beneath a light, I caught her wince and looked down to see a slight limp in her step. I'd seen her roll out of the trunk of that tiny, black sedan, but I'd missed whatever caused her ankle injury.

Wrapping an arm around her waist to offer better support, I tried to reassure her. "It's not much farther."

When we approached the house, I cringed.

Despite being a pretty normal two-story home for the area, it was obviously the home of bachelors. I couldn't help but wonder what she thought of its mildly depressing appearance.

The white and gray front porch held a bare, single light bulb. With no cover, the light shone in a small circle in front of the door. A moth fluttered around the bulb. We'd never given much thought to the entrance, and now, I wish we had. I wanted to make a good impression on Raegan, especially if she'd be around a lot.

I unlocked the door and pressed a hand to Raegan's back as we stepped through. Her trembling had increased, and a sob broke through the quiet.

Oh no, not good. She couldn't cry. I didn't do tears!

Yeah, okay, I had a little sister, but I'd only known about her in the last year. She never cried! What the hell should I do? I sucked in a breath and called on the reserves of calm that helped me through my sister's crisis last year.

"Come on." I flicked on the light in the small, tiled foyer, noticing again the plainness of the house.

Why didn't we bother to put a picture up or something?

I led her through to the kitchen, probably the most decorative room in the house. The cabinets were dark green with pale gray accents. The top ones featured stained glass fronts with one of four distinct designs, each representing a different element. A silver backsplash complemented the stainless-steel appliances, while red granite countertops ran across the L-shaped counters and the large island. A pale blue and white swirled tile was laid on the floor. Light pine stools were pushed against the island. Both the island and the counters were completely clear, unlike the large, pine table shoved against the far wall.

The table we were supposed to use for dining was currently covered with papers and books. We rarely ate there, and it showed.

Raegan sank onto a stool, tears streaking across her pretty, delicate features and deep, gulping breaths made her chest heave.

No, no, no. I couldn't handle this on my own.

Tarin! Tarin had sisters all his life. He'd know what to do.

I patted Raegan's shoulder. "I'll be right back. I'm gonna go find our first aid kit and my phone, okay? You're fine here, safe."

She let out a choked sob and threw her arms around my neck, clinging like a monkey in a tree. Warmth slid through me, and a funny, fluttery feeling rose in my stomach.

"Thank you." Her voice was nothing more than a breath in my ear.

Between that and the way her body pressed against mine, certain parts were starting to perk up and take notice. I pressed the ball of my tongue piercing against the roof of my mouth, hoping the discomfort would calm the situation, but that only made me wonder if she'd ever kissed a guy with a tongue piercing.

No, no, inappropriate, think of something else, anything else.

Praying she didn't notice my body's inappropriate reactions, I set her back on the stool. "I'll be right back."

I needed Tarin, or maybe River. Someone. Everything felt a bit sideways, and I didn't like it one

16

bit. I loved having a pretty girl in my arms, but this whole night was just weird.

Dashing up the stairs, I cracked Tarin's door. The steady beat of drums from his stereo, barely audible, greeted me as I slipped inside on silent feet and closed the door with a soft snick.

I put a hand on Tarin's shoulder and gave a gentle push on both his shoulder and the bond between us. "Tar? Wake up, man."

A hand shot out, smacking wildly at the air. A low, inaudible grumble came from the mounds of pillows on the bed.

"Tar! Come on! I have a weepy chick in our kitchen, and I need help!" I pushed against the bond again to express the urgency of the situation, then ducked the pillow that flew in my general direction.

Peering up, I found golden brown eyes glaring at me.

"What the frick do you want?" Tarin growled as he ran a mocha-colored hand over the dark fuzz on his head. He sounded like a bear whose hibernation I'd interrupted.

"Uh, there's this girl…"

"There's always a girl." Tarin sounded resigned as he crawled out of bed and yanked on a pair of sleep pants and a T-shirt that had been sitting, neatly folded, on the carved oak nightstand. "Gravy. Let's go see what kind of trouble you've found now."

I didn't blame Tarin for sounding a bit put out. I'd been known to bring my, uh, personal troubles to our doorstep for help more than once. There'd even been a rather big blow-up about it one night, when my personal trouble had brought her own personal trouble to our door. My Genus had been sore for a few days after that.

We'd barely crossed the threshold of the kitchen when I saw Tarin jerk suddenly.

Damn. I'd thought it was a fluke. *Hoped* it was a fluke.

"You felt it, didn't you?" I whispered, so Raegan wouldn't hear me. "The Iunctura?"

Tarin gave a barely perceptible nod, not taking his eyes from the weepy bundle of beauty sitting on a kitchen stool. Tarin moved toward her slowly, like he was approaching a terrified animal, making some low murmuring, nonsensical sounds that I thought were meant to soothe and calm.

It wasn't until Tarin's eyes widened at the sight of her split knuckles that I remembered the first aid kit. I dug under the sink for the one we kept in the kitchen.

"What the fuckin' shit!" I jerked back out of the

cabinet to find Zephyr, boxers barely clinging to his hips and ash brown hair hanging in his face, framed in the doorway to the kitchen glaring at me. "You bring another one of your little cunts home to get the hell beat out of us again?"

Fuck, fuck, fuck. Zephyr wasn't the most pleasant person at normal hours. Forget the middle of the night.

"Calm down, Zephyr!" I shot to my feet and dashed to intercept my angry friend, who was advancing on Raegan with his finger outstretched.

"Get the fuck out!" Zephyr yelled at her.

Raegan's tears fell faster, and she tumbled off the stool to the floor.

Tarin knelt beside her as I stepped in front of Zephyr and shoved against his chest, backing him out of the kitchen.

"Didn't you feel it?" I ground the words out as I finally got him into the hall. Maybe he hadn't registered the Iunctura because he wasn't fully awake yet.

"I felt it," he sneered, "but I don't give a shit what I felt! We're full. We have four. There ain't no fifth! Ain't no one heard of a fifth! So, I don't give a flying rat's ass what the flaming hell I felt. Whoever, *whatever* you brought in here tonight ain't fuckin' one of us!"

A pair of hands came down on Zephyr's shoulders, interrupting his tirade.

Spotting River, I breathed a sigh of relief.

"Calm down, Zephyr. I felt it, too. So did Ash, obviously. And I bet Tarin did, as well. It's odd, yes. We'll get answers soon." River's voice washed over us like a cool gush of water flowing, putting out Zephyr's anger.

He met my eyes over Zephyr's shoulder, letting me know that he'd deal with our angry friend.

Stepping back into the kitchen, I spot Raegan in a sobbing heap on Tarin's lap on the kitchen floor, her knuckles bandaged. From the evidence of Tarin's soaked shirt, she was having a pretty good cry, but Tarin didn't seem to care. He just rubbed his hands across her back as she clung to him. I wanted to help, but instead, I stood there feeling useless since Tarin had things handled.

River stepped into the kitchen. "I got Zephyr to head back to bed, let's deal with this."

His eyes found the heap of Tarin and Raegan, and he chuckled softly. He walked over, leaned down, and pulled Raegan from Tarin. She stiffened at first, though the flow of tears didn't stop. Her gaze roved his face before she finally relaxed into him. Her tears and sobs dried up quickly after that.

Damn. I didn't know River could do that.

"Hey, why don't you call someone to come get you?" River kept his voice soft and low as he handed her a phone. "I'm sure there's someone who's very worried about you."

Raegan tried to give River a smile as she took the phone and dialed, reminding me we hadn't called the cops yet, either.

"Hey, Devin, it's Rae," she said softly into the phone.

My curiosity about who she called got the better of me, and I stepped closer.

The irate tone of the person on the other end bothered me. Why the heck was this Devin guy yelling?

"Dee, I'm fine." Rae winced at the lie, and I chuckled. "I had a bit of a rescue." She rattled off the address River provided before saying bye.

"Hey," I spoke softly, hoping to avoid upsetting her again. "We should call the cops."

Raegan bit her lip, and damn, it was hot. It would be inappropriate to ask for her number, right? Right.

Finally, she nodded.

River stepped back into the hall as he placed the call.

It didn't take long before the doorbell rang.

Tarin answered it and led two guys into the kitchen. One was tall, dark, and full of tats and piercings. He appeared dangerous, but looks were often deceiving. The other one was shorter, with cropped, dark-blond hair and the start of a beard on his chin. He looked like he might have been Mr. Popular in school.

Rae flung herself at Mr. Popular, whose arms immediately held her close.

A little too close if anyone asked me.

"Pierson!" she cried.

"Hey, it's okay." The guy ran a hand down her hair, and I had the sudden, violent urge to snatch Raegan out of his arms.

"You're okay?" Worry laced her voice, sending another stab through my belly.

I really wanted this guy's hands off her.

"Thanks for taking care of my sister," Mr. Tattoo said. If handsy was Pierson, then Tattoo Guy must be Devin. "We should probably go."

"Not yet." River stepped back into the kitchen, phone still in hand. "The cops are on their way."

"Oh, damn. Yeah." Devin ran a hand across the

back of his neck. "Fuck. I was so worried about Rae that I'm not thinking straight."

He pulled Raegan from Pierson's arms and hugged her tight for a second before guiding her back to the stool.

At least, Pierson wasn't holding her anymore.

It didn't take long for the cops to arrive. As Raegan, Devin, and Pierson went through their story for them, I became more confused.

Why the obviously planned out, if poorly executed, kidnapping attempt on an ordinary girl? Of course, she couldn't actually be ordinary, not when we'd experienced Iunctura.

Raegan had gotten enough of a look at the guy who took her to describe him, which should help, but the whole thing still felt off. I really didn't like it.

Once the cops left, Devin pulled Raegan to her feet. "I should get her home. Thanks again."

He nodded at us and guided his sister out the door.

CHAPTER THREE

ASH

"Am I the only one who thinks just letting that girl walk out of here is nuts?" Tarin asked.

What the fuck was Tarin thinking? What were we gonna do, lock the girl up?

Tarin rolled his eyes. "I'm just saying we all felt Iunctura. It's not like that's easily breakable. We don't have her address or anything, and she supposedly belongs with us."

Well, damn. Maybe I should have asked for her number, but at least, we had her brother's number in River's phone.

"Sometimes you're a bunch of idiots." The growl came from the stairs.

I shot a glare at where Zephyr lounged against the

rail of the stairs. Hadn't he been grumpy enough for one night?

Zephyr rolled his eyes. "River, follow the fuckin' troublemaker. They got attacked once. Good chance they will again."

River slipped on his sneakers and headed out the door. A minute later, we heard his car start and head off.

Damn good thing we had that closet near the door. Did that thing have a name? I shook the thought off. That's what I got for not sleeping. It didn't matter what the closet was supposed to be called; we all tossed our shoes in there. Zephyr stalked across the kitchen, face still set in a scowl, and threw himself onto a stool. It tipped back dangerously before righting itself with a thud.

I winced, wondering if Zephyr had cracked the tile floor.

"I still don't think she's one of us. This is some kind of trick." He glared at me, but I wasn't about to let Grumpy Bear intimidate me.

I knew what I felt, and I knew what it meant. You'd think being a Ventus, Zephyr might be a little more relaxed. Apparently not, though. In the two years since Zephyr's Iunctura, I'd rarely seen the guy smile.

I didn't care if Zephyr thought it was all a trick. Raegan was sweet and gorgeous. I really wanted to get to know her, and I'd take it any way I could get it.

Zephyr did have a point, though. I'd grown up in the Elementum world, attended Illustratio Academy, the private Elementum school, and I couldn't remember anything about a fifth element.

I sought out the burnished gold of Tarin's eyes and silently asked him if he'd ever heard of a fifth.

Tarin shrugged. "I think I vaguely remember some story that was referenced at school."

"Maybe we should call our folks and ask them?" My gaze drifted to the clock on the microwave as I asked the question.

Shit, it was the middle of the night. I kind of forgot about that for a minute.

"Mom and Dad will murder me if I call and wake up Aurae." Tarin chuckled ruefully.

That just left Dad. At least, my sister was old enough to ignore a middle-of-the-night call. Hell, she might not even be home.

I grabbed my phone off the counter and dialed, hoping dad wasn't on shift tonight.

"Phoenix," the barely audible grumble came across the line.

"Hey, Dad, it's Ash."

"Considering my daughter is sound asleep in her room, I'm pretty sure I could have figured that out, even at this time of night. What's up, Firebrand?" I heard muttering, then, "It's just Ash, go back to sleep."

Damn, I'd woken Kelly, my dad's fiancé. I seriously envied the way Dad could go from zombie to fully functional adult in like a half a second without coffee.

Restless, I paced as I talked. Tarin's and Zephyr's eyes followed me, likely wondering if I was gonna burn a trench into the floor...again. "Sorry for waking up Kelly, but um, there was this girl."

I ran a hand through the blond tips of my brown hair and flinched at how that sounded. Dad would think the same thing Tarin said earlier: There was always a girl. Dad would understand, though. Ignis were passionate by nature, and before Kelly, dad rarely had an empty bed.

"She sorta...rolled into me." I paced faster. "Out of the trunk of a car. She was pretty banged up, split knuckles and some serious bruising."

"You don't need me for first aid, kiddo. You can handle that." Dad sounded like he was trying to go back to sleep.

"No, it's not first aid I need you for. It's

information. Elementum information," I said before he hung up. "Dad, Iunctura occurred. We all felt it."

"Put me on speaker. Now!" I jumped at Dad's firm tone. He was for sure awake now.

As I put him on speakerphone, the front door opened. River came in and sank into a chair. "Followed them to the house and waited until she was inside. She's good for the night." Tossing a paper down on the table, he leaned forward. "Wrote down the address."

I nodded, then turned back to the phone "Okay, Dad. Speaker is on."

"Everyone there and awake?" he demanded in a tone that took control of the situation.

A chorus of, "Yes, sir," went up.

"Are you guys sure? You all felt the Iunctura?" Dad asked.

Again, a chorus of, "Yes, sir."

"Did any of you tell the other beforehand?" he continued the interrogation. "Did you all feel it at once?"

"I felt it first," I replied. "But I didn't say anything."

Glances were shared between Tarin, River, and Zephyr.

"I think the rest of us all felt it at the same time," Tarin answered for them.

"Did any of you feel a Foederis?" Dad asked.

I shot the others a concerned glance, but everyone shook their heads. Thank the elements. A broken bond was a terrible thing to experience.

"No," I responded for all of us.

"So, no Foederis but Iunctura. Odd. That would make her a fifth, but…." Dad muttered to himself, thinking out loud.

No one said a word. We barely dared to breathe.

"Five… A Fifth… But what element…" A sharp note entered his voice. "Wait, the Quintus Myth?"

Come on, Dad, you have a memory like a steel trap.

"Okay, guys, just hang tight for a couple days," he instructed. "I need to call Maybelle, and you know the Sages can be hard to get a hold of."

Tarin sat up straighter, eyes wide. "Why do you need to call Mammy?"

Maybelle was Tarin's grandmother, and he'd never heard of this myth? Weird.

"Because I'm pretty sure she's the one who told me the Quintus Myth when I was a kid," he explained. "I don't remember the story, though."

Wait, dad didn't remember something? I couldn't think of the last time that had happened.

"I know it's a bit odd, but I was pretty little, and I ain't exactly getting younger," he grumbled. "A few old memories are bound to slip. Now, stop worrying and get back to sleep, boys."

"Yes, sir. Good night, sir," I cringed when we spoke in unison again.

Shit, what was up with that? Fluke of being up this late, maybe?

"Night, boys." Dad clicked off, leaving us to head to bed and ponder the conversation.

Unlike earlier in the evening, exhaustion took over now, and I dropped off quickly.

Clarity and answers didn't come with the breaking of the dawn. The pink, orange, and purple streaks across the horizon didn't bring any sudden revelations or miraculous phone calls. The beams of sunlight streaking through soft, pale gray clouds didn't reveal the previous evening to have been a dream or delusion.

If anything, the rising sun brought with it a certainty that everything had changed. I felt the others more strongly across the bond than I ever had before, and I could feel Raegan, a lingering presence on the fringes of the bond.

Stumbling downstairs, I walked blindly into the kitchen, grabbed the mug someone was holding, and sank onto a stool as I sipped.

Scalding coffee burned its way down, sweet and creamy, just the way I liked it. I shuddered and breathed a sigh of relief as the sweet nectar worked through my system, caffeine flowing into my bloodstream.

The mug was nearly empty when I noticed River smirking at me as he leaned back against the counter.

I scowled at him.

"Don't you have somewhere to be, Fish?" I muttered as I got up for a refill.

River was a swim coach at a local high school.

River laughed. "Summer vacation, Ash."

"Fucker," I muttered into my fresh coffee.

"Be nice, Ash," Tarin admonished as he came in from the backyard.

Crazy ass would have been out at first light in his garden.

"I was thinking, maybe we should go see Raegan," Tarin added. "She didn't seem to feel what happened last night. I'm starting to wonder if she even knows about Elementum."

"If we're visiting the troublemaker, we need to do it this morning. I have tours scheduled this afternoon." Zephyr scowled from the stairs.

Apparently, he still had a stick up his ass about Raegan.

I flipped him off, mostly just because, and took another sip of coffee.

No one really said anything while we all grabbed coffee or breakfast because, just like that, we'd decided to go see Raegan. We were all pretty different, personality-wise, but we meshed and balanced perfectly. I loved that about my Genus. How would a fifth change us? Would it screw with our dynamic?

We moved around each other flawlessly, things being passed before they were even asked for, dishes rinsed and in the dishwasher, counters wiped.

By the time we finished, the kitchen was flawless again. Zephyr wouldn't have it any other way, and we'd learned early on to keep things clean. Zephyr in a tear over the state of the house was definitely not something any of us wanted to live through again.

With breakfast dealt with, we piled into River's old SUV. The thing was freakin' ancient, but it ran beautifully and had been the right price when River needed a car.

Since it was the only vehicle big enough to hold

us all and River knew where we were going, it made sense to take it. Thank all the Elements he'd written down her address when he followed her home.

The drive wasn't long, and soon, we pulled up in front of a blue-gray, two-story house. All the windows were open, and the sheer, white curtains fluttered a bit in the breeze. It was clear and sunny, promising to be a gorgeous summer day.

A petite blond answered our knock with a grin that lit up her whole face, and a musical southern drawl graced our ears. "Well, hello, boys. What can I do for y'all?"

A head of dark hair passed by the doorway, and Devin peered out before turning for the stairs. "Those are the guys who found Rae last night, Mom."

"Hi, ma'am." River and his never fail charm-a-parent-mode kicked into action. "We just wanted to make sure Raegan was okay. She seemed really shaken up last night."

"Well, come on in. I'm Jaleene Corwin."

We introduced ourselves and followed her into a large, sunny kitchen. Soft, buttery yellows and sparkling whites helped make the space seem spacious and well-lit. I made a beeline for the coffeepot. Two cups weren't enough. A wooden stand held white mugs next to the coffeepot and two small, round, yellow containers proved to hold sugar and powdered creamer when I looked.

The coffee was warm, but I preferred coffee just this side of burning off taste buds, so I sent a little shot of warmth into the mug as I stirred. Steam curled into the air as I turned to the others, wondering why everyone was so quiet.

A glance around the room showed Mrs. Corwin with wide eyes, staring at my mug.

Well, shit. My foggy brain hadn't really thought through my actions.

"You... You're like Raegan, aren't you?" she asked softly, as if she didn't want anyone overhearing.

I exchanged a glance with the others to figure out how to respond. We didn't know what she knew, so playing dumb seemed the way to go.

"What do you mean, Mrs. Corwin?" River asked her.

She waved at the table and sat as she spoke again. "You have...are...um…elements? Abilities?"

We shared another concerned look as we joined her.

She didn't sound like she even really knew what her daughter was. How was that possible?

"Mrs. Corwin, we're a bit confused. You sound

unsure about exactly what Raegan is." River leaned forward.

Mrs. Corwin sighed. "I'm not entirely sure, to be honest. Raegan and Devin are adopted. Raegan's adoption occurred a bit differently than Devin's, though. We had just started talking about looking for a little girl. Devin had recently turned four, and we thought it might be a good time. One night, there was a knock on our back door. We were both surprised to find an older gentleman holding a tiny bundle wrapped in a pink blanket. He told us she was special and extremely rare in his society. He called her the Quintus and asked us to raise her and protect her, said he needed a family outside the element…Elementum?"

She looked at us when she said it, and we nodded to confirm. "That she was being hunted, and he didn't know who to trust. Then he disappeared, quite literally in front of our eyes. I don't even know what her element is. We kept waiting for her powers to show, but it's never happened."

She turned a hopeful gaze on us.

"Mrs. Corwin, I'm afraid we don't have many answers for you, yet," Tarin spoke up. "What we can tell you is that she is one of us, and from what we can tell, she belongs in our Genus, our group. That means everything to us. Ideally, we'd want her to be with us, in our home, and begin training right away, but am I correct in assuming that she doesn't know any of this?"

Since the others had things well in hand, I sat back and enjoyed my heavenly drink.

"We were going to tell her when her powers showed, but…" Mrs. Corwin shrugged.

It wasn't hard to understand. If Raegan's powers never showed, she probably wouldn't believe her parents. It made the whole situation harder. Her power was obviously still dormant, and if she wouldn't have believed her parents, she sure as hell wasn't going to believe us. We needed to approach this very carefully.

Slower might be better in this case.

"I think we should hold off on saying anything right away. We have people who might have answers." I set the now empty mug down as I spoke. "Let's wait 'til then. For now, we'll just try to be her friends."

Steps sounded on the stairs, and I glanced over my shoulder to see who it was.

My breath caught in my throat. Raegan headed down the stairs in a pair of dark wash jeans that hugged every mouthwatering curve and an orange lace tank top that barely met the waistband of her jeans. A simple gold headband adorned with white flowers held back her white hair.

"Mornin', sweetie," Mrs. Corwin called. "Come on down. Those nice boys from last night came to check on you."

Rae froze, and her head turned so fast I worried she might give herself whiplash.

Instead, her eyes widened, and pink rose to her cheeks when she spotted us. With a horrified squeak, she turned and ran back up the stairs.

She tried, anyway.

Instead, she made it up about two steps, tripped, and went down face first.

The second I saw her miss the step, I shot out of my chair and raced over to check on her. I wasn't the only one, either. River and Tarin both joined us.

The need to make sure a virtual stranger was okay wasn't strange for us. Part of being in a Genus meant an ingrained need to protect the other members. The strange bit was that Zephyr was able to come only halfway to the stairs before he stopped and crossed his arms over his chest, scowling at Rae.

I pulled a stammering Rae to her feet and ran my hands over her to check for injuries. Tarin tried to pull her into his arms as River rubbed her back.

"Oh, for fuck's sake, you idiots, let the girl

breathe," Zephyr called from the bottom of the stairs.

Anger flared through me, and I turned in his direction. "What do you care? You called her a cunt last night."

Zephyr flinched. "Uh, yeah. Sorry about that, troublemaker. I was running on no sleep and extra grouchy."

I wasn't sure if Rae heard, since she yanked herself from our hands at that moment and continued her race up the stairs.

A minute later, we heard a door slam.

I shared a look with Tarin and River before following her and knocking on her door.

"Go away!" she cried from the other side. "And tell Zephyr it's fine."

"Come on, baby," I pleaded. "Don't hide. It was cute."

The faint sound of a groan came through the door, followed by a firm, "No. Go away."

With a sigh, I gave up and headed back to the stairs to rejoin the others.

Yep. We were off to a great start.

CHAPTER FOUR

RAEGAN

"You didn't." Pierson stared at me in disbelief from his seat in my desk chair.

A few days had passed since my epic embarrassment in front of the guys who saved me, and I'm still appalled by my actions.

On the bed, I hugged my pillow against my chest. "Yep, I totally did."

"No way." He shook his head. "I don't believe you."

"Believe it," I insisted, my face heating from mortification. "It was horrible."

He squinted at me. "You're jerking my chain, right?"

I shook my head. "Nope."

"But you wouldn't." He squinted harder, as if I

DESI LIN

had transformed into a new person. "I mean, you've never done something like that before."

"I know!" I wailed.

"But...how?" He shook his head. "I mean... What?"

"I don't know!" I fell back on my bed to stare at the ceiling. "It was like one minute I was perfectly fine, then they looked at me, and I lost all control over my body."

"Oh God, that must have been…" He trailed off, searching for the right word.

"Horrible, humiliating, heinous…" I offered.

Pierson clapped. "Nice use of alliteration."

"Shut up." Sitting up, I threw the pillow at him.

He caught it easily and tossed it back before standing from the chair to mess with the stuff on my dresser. He leaned forward, peering into the antique mirror that hung above it.

"So…" he asked.

"I don't know." I kept my gaze fixed on my white comforter, picking at imaginary lint. "I haven't seen or heard from them since. I think maybe I scared them off."

"Isn't that a good thing, though?" he asked gently. "I mean, didn't you say they kind of gave you a weird, funny feeling?"

Heat crawled up my cheeks. How did I explain that it was a good weird, funny feeling? My disappointment over how they seemed to have forgotten me was hard enough to admit. I definitely didn't want to tell Pierson about the dreams. He'd completely lose it.

Pierson turned from the mirror as I lifted my gaze.

"Oh. My. God. What did you do?" Laughter burst out of me, and I chucked another pillow at him. "Go wash your face, you freak!"

Pierson cocked a hip out, put one hand on it, and batted his now heavily lined eyes at me.

"What, you don't like the guyliner?" He pouted a lip out.

I laughed harder and buried my face in my hands.

The clod of combat boots in the hall made us both turn toward the door as Devin strode into view.

He glanced our way, stopped, then grinned at Pierson.

"Whoa, looking good, Pier." Devin winked at him and continued to his room.

"See? Dee likes it," Pierson said smugly.

I rolled my eyes. "Go wash your face."

Pierson threw his hands up in mock exasperation as he headed toward the connected bathroom.

"How come he gets away with it?" Pierson's question echoed off the white tile of the bathroom.

"Because it looks good on him," I replied.

Pierson sighed with appreciation. "Yeah, it does."

I didn't think I was supposed to hear that, so I didn't say anything.

Pierson came back into the room, face freshly washed, and plopped on the bed. "Okay, so tell me the whole story."

I shot him a glare. "Once wasn't enough?"

"We never got all the way through it," Pierson pointed out as he leaned against the mound of fluffy, brightly colored throw pillows that were spread across the bed. They were the only color on the all-white bedding.

Pierson spread his legs out and patted the bed in between them.

I crawled over, settling between Pierson's open legs and leaning back against his chest.

He wrapped his arms around my shoulders and squeezed gently. "Okay, come on. Give me the whole embarrassing debacle from the beginning."

"I can't believe you're making me relive it." Leaning against Pierson's arm, I closed my eyes. "I didn't know they were here. Hell, I still don't know how they knew where I lived. I was just going to grab coffee—"

"Wait." Pierson held up a hand. "Which pajamas were you wearing? The tiny little shorts that barely cover your ass and that white tank that's practically see-through and cut so low you're in danger of releasing the girls if you breathe too much?"

I tried to shoot him another glare over my shoulder but settled for smacking his arm instead, then cuddling back into his embrace. "I was dressed, now hush. So, Mom says something, and I look over to find all four of them at the table with Mom, staring at me."

"And that's when you squeaked? You actually squeaked? And ran?" Disbelief laced Pierson's voice.

At the memory of sounding like a freakin' mouse or one of those yappy little rat dogs, heat rose in my cheeks again. I didn't think I'd ever forget what happened after that, either. "Yes, I squeaked. I don't know what came over me! I just squeaked, turned, ran back up the stairs, tripped on fucking *air*, and fell face-first into the stairs!"

The fucker I called my best friend shook with laughter.

No worries, I'd get revenge.

"I could actually hear them running over, and

when I looked up, they were all standing around me. Well, not Zephyr. But then they were helping me up and running their hands over me, and I…" I cut myself off before I revealed exactly how hot and bothered I'd been from the guys' hands all over me. "I, uh, ran to my room."

It was true enough. I'd even slammed the door and refused to come out, too embarrassed to face the guys.

"I'm sure it wasn't nearly as bad as you remember it." Pierson gave me a gentle, reassuring squeeze, but I could still hear the laughter in his voice.

He was totally getting pranked. I'd have to come up with something good. Maybe I could get Devin to draw something totally embarrassing and make Pierson think it was a tattoo.

"Pierson, hon, are your folks home yet?" Mom asked from the doorway.

Pierson's parents traveled a lot, and Mom hated that Pierson was left on his own so much.

"Not 'til Wednesday, Mrs. C," he answered.

"You'll be staying the night, then?" Mom made it sound like a suggestion, but we both knew it was actually an order. She wasn't about to let Pierson go home to an empty house. "Raegan, sweetie, can you give me a hand in the kitchen?"

I stifled a groan as I got up to follow mom. This could not be good. Mom had her *talking* tone on.

Down in the kitchen, Mom set me to chopping vegetables while she prepped the crust and chicken for her famous, homemade chicken pot pies. We worked quietly for a while, only the sound of the music drifting out of the nearby speakers filled the silence.

"Rae, honey, about those boys from the other night," Mom eventually said, revealing her sudden need for my culinary assistance.

Oh boy, here it comes.

"Do they know about Pierson?" she asked tentatively.

Huh? That wasn't what I was expecting.

"What are you talking about, Mom?" I looked at her in confusion. "I barely met them."

Mom set aside the crust she'd been working on and wiped her floury hands on the white, waffle weave towel that hung from her belt loop.

She closed the few steps between us and pushed at a lock of white hair that had fallen into my eyes. "It's just you and Pierson, you're so close, and I can't help but worry that he might get a little jealous of other guys paying so much attention to you. I'm pretty sure at least one of them was interested, and it seems like you might be spending a lot of time with them."

"Doubtful. It's not like they've contacted me since then." I couldn't keep the disappointment from my voice.

Mom hummed like she knew something but was keeping it to herself. "All I'm saying, sweetie, is maybe you should make sure they know you have a boyfriend."

Wait… What?

The knife clattered on the countertop, narrowly missing my fingers. Mom thought Pierson and I were dating? Oh God, so many weird things made sense now. Oh, if only she knew.

I couldn't help but burst out laughing. "Oh my God, Mom, Pierson and I aren't dating. It's not like that. We're just friends."

It was Mom's turn to look confused. "But I thought… Oh."

She seemed to deflate a bit, and I wrapped my arms around her and squeezed tight.

Mom squeezed back, then pulled away, a blush spreading across her face. "Well, don't I feel silly. But whyever not? Don't you find him attractive? Doesn't he think you're pretty?"

I chuckled softly. "Yes to both. Pierson is very

handsome, and anyone would be lucky to be dating him, but I'm not exactly his type, Mom."

I held my breath and waited for her to ask who was then. It was a question I couldn't answer, at least not until Pierson actually told me. Fortunately, feet on the stairs prevented the inevitable.

Pierson popped into the kitchen on a dash, skidding to a halt next to Mom and pecking her on the cheek.

"I'll be right back, Mrs. C. I need to grab my soccer gear from the house. Tomorrow, I'm supposed to meet up with the guys for practice." He glanced at the counter and groaned. "Oh man, chicken pot pies. My favorite."

Pierson dashed by me on his way to the door and popped a kiss on my forehead.

Mom shot me a look, complete with a raised eyebrow.

I shook my head.

Pierson skirted around Dad coming in the door. "Hey, Mr. C, chicken pot pie for dinner. Be right back."

"How are the two most beautiful women in the world?" Dad grinned wide as he dropped a quick kiss on the top of my head before giving mom a prolonged hello.

I sighed as I watched them. They were so happy together, so much in love, even after all these years. They hadn't had the easiest start, either. I hoped that when I found love, I would be as happy as they were.

"You know, it's awesome that you guys love each other so much, but could we maybe skip the live make-out sessions when you come home?" Devin teased as he walked into the kitchen.

I shot him a glare.

"What? I'm just saying, some of us might not want to watch."

"You better watch out, sport. I can still take you in b-ball," Dad mock-threatened as he went up the stairs.

"Not a chance, old man!" Devin called after him, looked around the kitchen, then frowned. "Where's Pier?"

I bit back the silly grin that threatened to break free.

"He went to grab his soccer stuff," Mom replied. "Apparently, he has practice tomorrow."

Devin turned back in my direction before continuing, "Pier is playing tomorrow? Sweet. I'll have to go watch."

"It's just an informal practice, Dee," I informed him.

Why would he want to go watch Pierson practice?

"Yeah, I know." Devin shrugged in an absentminded way.

What was up with him?

"When you see those nice boys again, you should invite them for a barbecue," Mom said suddenly. "We could have it next Saturday, after you get off work."

I looked at her like she was crazy. Didn't I just tell her I probably wasn't going to see them again?

"Is Mom trying to set you up for a date?" Devin teased as he pulled himself up onto the counter.

My cheeks heated, and I threw some veggies at him.

Laughing, he caught them and popped a carrot into his mouth, his combat boots banging against the cabinets.

A loud crash and a clatter drew my attention to the door where Pierson had barreled back in and dropped his bag.

"Hey." He scanned the room as he entered, taking in the scene.

Mom was just putting the pies in the oven. There was a heavy sprinkling of flour over everything and a pile of dishes in the sink.

Then, the speakers blasted to life with an old, slow country song.

Dad came down the stairs, grabbed Mom's hand, and spun her into his arms, dancing her around the kitchen.

Devin grinned and hopped off the counter, grabbing my hand and pulling me into a dance with him.

For a moment, I worried Pierson would feel left out, but when I glanced over Devin's shoulder, it was to find Pierson cutting in on Mom and Dad.

They grinned and opened their arms to him, forming a trio as they danced across the kitchen.

Man, I loved my nutty family.

CHAPTER FIVE

TARIN

our pen really stinks. I shot the mental message to the large, mixed-breed dog the shelter owners called Horse.

Forever Home was a small, independent shelter. They got some funding through sales of accessories and food when animals were adopted. They did several fundraisers throughout the year, but they largely relied on volunteers to supplement the rather tiny, full-time staff.

Everyone who worked and volunteered at the shelter was totally committed and adored the animals. I'd been volunteering here since I was fourteen, but it took a while before I could handle going into the pens. As long as I didn't stay in them too long, I was okay.

Horse cocked his head and continued panting lightly, just staring as I scrubbed out his pen.

Horse was an appropriate name. None of us had been able to figure out exactly what mix of breeds Horse was. He was huge, though, and most of the shelter staff figured he had some very large breed in him. The thing was, he was also a bit on the shaggy side, making him look more like an overgrown stuffed animal than an actual dog.

He was sweet and good-natured, but we quickly discovered that he was shy. The only time we could coax him out of the pen and into the exercise area was if it was empty. He wouldn't leave so we could clean it, either.

While many people showed interest in him, Horse was reluctant to spend time with families he didn't know. I remained one of the few volunteers he interacted with.

Of course, it helped to be able to talk to him. Normally, Horse was very excitable when I came in, but he seemed extra quiet today.

What's up, big guy? I asked as I set the scrub brush into the nearby bucket of suds, then hauled it into the hall.

Grabbing up the hose I'd left curled like a snake

on the floor, I twisted it on and took it back into the pen to rinse it off.

The family was here again.

I learned early that animals had different levels of communication, depending on their circumstances. Most wild animals used pictures to communicate, though some simply used their own language. I'd never quite figured out if that was because they couldn't use pictures or they were just too lazy. Domestic animals, though, usually had some level of human speech, most likely because they picked it up from their owners.

A couple days ago, a family had come by and shown a great deal of interest in Horse, even though no one could coax him out of his pen for a visit. Apparently, they were still interested.

Wouldn't that be a good thing? Don't you want a family? I asked him.

Horse sank to the floor, resting his head on his paws and gazing dolefully at me.

I wanted to give him a treat, even though I knew I wasn't supposed to. I couldn't resist those eyes.

Yes, but it means no more Tarin.

Oh, dear, sweet dog.

I crouched, ensuring the hose was aimed away, and gave Horse a quick scratch behind one shaggy, brown ear. *Aw, buddy. I love you, too. I'd take you home if I could.*

Having four roommates—well, more like brothers, really—meant that something like a pet had to be approved by everyone. Ash had met Horse and loved him, but I didn't know if River and Zephyr would want such a large animal around.

I stood, forcing myself to ignore his whine as I shut off the water. *Give the family a chance, okay? Try going into the play area next time they're here.*

Horse gave a soft snuff that I knew meant he was agreeing.

I set Horse's pen back to rights and filled his bowls.

As I was putting away the cleaning supplies, a familiar voice reached my ears. "Hey, Horse. How are you today, sweetheart?"

I dashed around the corner—thankfully, Horse's pen was on the end—to find Raegan crouched down and scratching Horse's ear. A grin broke over my face. We'd wanted to give her time to recover from her near kidnapping before we shook her world up again.

"Hey." My grin widened as she tried to spin in her crouched position but ended up on her butt instead. I held out a hand, which she gratefully accepted, and pulled her to her feet.

"H…H…Hi," Raegan stammered out, a beautiful blush spreading across her fair skin.

I liked the way she looked with a blush. I might have to make it happen more often.

"Um, you're, um…" she floundered, obviously not remembering my name.

Her awkwardness was kind of adorable.

"Tarin," I provided helpfully. "Did you come in to adopt a pet? Horse is a great choice."

Raegan shook her head.

A tugging made me look down to find I still held her hand. Surprisingly, I didn't want to let go. But that would be super awkward, so I dropped it. No need to seem like a weirdo creeper or something.

"I, um, volunteer here on Saturdays." The more she stumbled when she spoke, the redder she got.

I wanted to stroke her cheek and see if I could calm the redness. Instead, I tucked my hands into the pockets of my khaki cargo shorts.

"I'm surprised I haven't run into you before." Because I definitely would have remembered her. "Come on, let's go see what else is on the agenda today."

Her eyes widened, and she made that squeaking sound she'd made the day we'd gone to see her. Figuring she was about five seconds from bolting, I grabbed her hand and tugged her in the direction of the volunteer room.

We hadn't wanted to overwhelm or spook Rae, so we'd let her be for a few days. An attempted abduction was bound to leave a mark on the emotions, after all.

Now, though, we worked side-by-side, scrubbing out pens and helping exercise the animals for a couple hours. We didn't talk much, but I didn't mind and figured it meant she was comfortable in my presence. I spent most of the time trying to figure out how we should move forward with her. We needed to get her used to being with us, especially since she would eventually need to move in with us.

Her family were Norms, which meant that she had no idea what she was or what she could do. She knew nothing about our world. We'd have to tread carefully.

It was odd, though, how comfortable I felt around her. I'd never had issues when it came to dating, but growing up with three sisters left me with a tendency to be quietly annoyed by a lot of typical feminine behaviors, most particularly their verbal diarrhea.

Raegan didn't seem to feel the need to fill the silence with random, meaningless chitchat, which I appreciated. There was a certain beauty in silence. It allowed one to really focus on the world around them, rather than on their own selfish desires.

We'd just finished up the cats' litter pans when an idea hit me.

Shoving the pan I'd filled with fresh litter back into the pen, I brushed a hand across Raegan's arm to get her attention.

Her cheeks flushed bright red again as she turned in my direction.

"So, the guys and I had plans to head over to Strawberry Lanes. Wanna join us?" I asked.

Raegan blinked a few times, like she couldn't quite believe I invited her to join in. "Okay, sure."

No awkward stumbling this time. I kind of missed it.

"Sweet. Do you need to grab anything from the volunteer room?" When she shook her head, I backed toward the employee-only area. "I'm going to go grab my things out of the locker. Meet you out front?"

She nodded in agreement, and I headed into the volunteer room, which was about as plain as a room could get. White walls held a few posters and pictures randomly tacked up by volunteers. A single, small countertop held a coffeepot and microwave, the cabinet underneath storing the supplies and mugs for it. Tucked into the corner was a plain, white fridge, and a small row of black, metal lockers covered the other wall. Folding chairs surrounded a simple, round table in the center of the room to give people a place to sit.

Opening the locker I stowed my wallet and cell in earlier, I grabbed both and swiped open my phone. I needed to let the others know what was happening.

Tarin: Ran into Raegan. Invited her to join us at Strawberry Lanes.

River: We're going bowling?

Zephyr: What the fuck?

Ash: I guess we are now.

Zephyr: You guys better be glad I love you. Fuckin' bowling. Really?

Tarin: It was all I could come up with!

Ash: It might be fun. Been ages since I went bowling.

River: We'll meet you there, Tarin.

Grinning and shaking my head at my friends, I made my way out to the parking lot, where Raegan waited. A glance around revealed her leaning against the exterior wall, arms crossed over her chest, her eyes closed and looking lost in thought.

I gently stroked her arm to get her attention.

Bad idea.

She jumped backward, sending herself into the red brick of the building, screeching as her skin scraped against it. Attempting to right herself, she overcorrected, losing her balance, and headed for a nice, hard butt plant on the concrete.

Well, ship.

Jumping in front of her, I wrapped my arms around her waist to steady her as she regained her balance. Her odd but beautiful white hair had fallen into her face, and she tried to move it by blowing it out of the way.

I couldn't help the silent chuckles.

"Don't do that to a girl!" She shot a glare at me. "Don't you know how to make noise when you walk? If we're going to spend any more time together, I might have to sew bells on your toes."

I didn't even try to stop the laughter at the image that produced. I could just imagine walking around with tiny gold Christmas bells attached to each toe, like I was perpetually wearing elf shoes or something.

Raegan pulled out of my arms, still glaring. "Go ahead, yuck it up. I only could have cracked my head open, you know. No big deal."

I honestly tried to stop laughing, but she looked so cute with all that fake righteous indignation, stray hairs still falling across her face, foot tapping against the concrete. Hastily sucking in air, I tried again to collect myself.

After a few gulping breaths, I managed to stop, though a grin still graced my face.

I glanced around the parking lot. "Do you want to follow me? Or I can drive you there and bring you back later to pick up your car."

"My brother dropped me off earlier. If you don't mind driving me, that would be great." She pulled out her phone. "Let me just tell him I have a ride."

I wait while she sends her text, and as soon as she tucks her phone away, I grabbed her hand and led her to where I'd parked the truck.

It wasn't anything fancy. A white Chevy, a few years old, with Washington Landscaping in large green letters down the sides, the phone number below it. Technically, it was dad's truck, but there were two that were used for the landscaping business, so it wasn't usually a problem for me to borrow one.

Actually, most of the time, this one was with me, anyway, since I helped out regularly. It made things a lot easier when someone could shift the dirt around with a flick of a finger.

I opened the door, helped her up into the truck, jogged around to my door, hopped in, then started up the truck, its engine roaring. As I headed toward the bowling alley, a comfortable silence descended again.

God, I could get used to this.

A few minutes later, I pulled into a space in the rear of the lot, then rounded the truck to help Raegan down. Glancing around, I spotted Ash's bike and River's Bronco.

Good, the others were already here.

CHAPTER SIX

RAEGAN

We pushed through the doors to an assault on my senses. Bowling alleys weren't new to me, but that first step was always a shock. I scanned the bowling alley, looking anxiously for Ash.

I ended up finding River and Zephyr first. They had made a big impact on me the first night we met for completely different reasons. River for being so kind and comforting me while I cried, and Zephyr for yelling.

The two stood side-by-side near the shoe counter, Zephyr leaning into River. It was the first time I'd seen them next to each other, and I suddenly realized what a striking pair they made. They were nearly the same height, though River appeared to be an inch taller. River wore his black hair close cropped, while Zephyr's rich brown locks hung around his face. They were both lean, but Zephyr was definitely smaller and thinner, with River possessing the kind of defined muscle seen on Olympic swimmers on TV. His sea green eyes perfectly complimented Zephyr's storm blue ones. They were beautiful together.

We made our way to the counter where River and Zephyr stood, and we all grabbed shoes. As we made our way to the lane we'd been assigned, I looked around again for Ash.

I really hoped he was coming. I felt like we had a special connection, maybe because of the way he took care of me when I'd been kidnapped. Cliche, I knew, and I wasn't blind to the tiny crush I was developing.

"If you're looking for Ash, try the snack bar," a soft voice whispered into my ear.

I jumped, which of course meant I tripped on air and headed for a rather elegant face plant.

Strong arms wrapped around my waist and stopped the inevitable.

A glance back revealed my savior to be River. "Sorry, thought you knew I was there."

Heat rose on my cheeks as my stomach dropped. Could I be more awkward? What the hell was up with that? What was it about these guys that had me tripping on air?

Shaking my head, I turned toward the snack bar and easily spotted Ash. His tousled, brown-blond locks and edgy clothes made him stand out among the more conservative people. He stood at the counter, and as I watched, he shifted, giving me a view of the counter girl flirting with him.

Queasiness rolled through me when Ash flirted back, and a low, unconscious growl escaped my lips.

"Did you just growl?" River chuckled in my ear, reminding me he still held me.

And now, I realized my fingers had been stroking his arms, tracing the swirled wave tattoo. What the fuck was up with me?

"Sorry." With my blush deepening, I stepped out of his hold.

Another glance at Ash showed him and the girl still flirting. She looked around the same age as me, but younger than River and Zephyr.

Reminded I knew nothing about them, I returned my attention to the others. "Hey, how old are you guys?"

River chuckled, and his eyebrows drew together. "Random, I like it. Zephyr and I are twenty-three, Tarin and Ash are twenty-one. Why?"

"Curiosity," I said with a shrug.

"Hey, you two gonna cuddle all night, or are we gonna bowl?" Zephyr called from where he and Tarin stood by the ball return.

As we made our way over, I noticed that Tarin and Zephyr had collected balls, set up the scoreboard, and gotten everything ready while I'd been getting all weird about Ash and River.

My tight muscles relaxed, and I smiled wide, ready to have a little fun.

Ash strode over with a tray of drinks and snacks and set them on a table just outside the lane area. His eyes lit up when they landed on me, which sent my insides quivering.

Stupid tiny crush.

He rushed over, threw an arm around me, and tugged me into a sideways hug. "Hey, how are you feeling? No more crazies stuffing you into trunks?"

I hugged him back, burying my face against his neck. Somehow, he smelled a bit like a bonfire.

The hug lasted only a heartbeat before Tarin corralled us all to the lanes.

Before long, the guys had me laughing at their antics and jokes like we'd known each other for years. It was easy to see how close they were. I felt honored that they had invited me to join them tonight. I hadn't bowled in ages, and it turned out I really sucked.

"Someone needs lessons," Zephyr grumped.

I glanced over at him to find him glaring at me, arms crossed over his chest. Even though the others welcomed me, I still hadn't broken through his icy exterior.

Ash took pity on me and followed when my turn came up.

He gave me tips and helped me figure out how to stand and stuff like that, but my mind was only half paying attention since his hands were all over me. No matter how innocent it was, I still felt my face burning.

Eventually, he stepped back, and I threw the ball.

It soared down the lane and hit the pins with a resounding crack. Amazed, I watched as every pin fell.

"Did you see?" I spun to face Ash, a giggle escaping as I bounced around, almost crossing over into the next lane. "Did you? I knocked them all down! All of them!"

Ash grabbed my waist, attempting to stop my craziness. "Yes, baby, I saw it. Calm down before you break something."

A hand stroked down my back that didn't belong

to Ash, and a glance over my shoulder revealed Tarin as the one gently rubbing circles.

Something about the action grounded me, and within moments, I stopped bouncing and just glowed with happiness.

"Coach Creedence!" called a soft, feminine voice.

Tarin and Ash quickly stepped away from me, and for half a second, I mourned the loss of their touch.

A pretty, short-haired brunette, who couldn't have been more than sixteen, came to a screeching halt in front of River.

Was he Coach Creedence?

River gave the girl a small smile, and I noticed he was careful to keep an obvious distance between them. "Hey, Laura. What's up?"

"The girls and I were wondering if you managed to get some pool time for the team." She points back to where more girls the same age hovered nearby. "I really want to work on my butterfly, and Amber wants to improve her freestyle time."

River shook his head, though he was still smiling. "You girls are always wanting to practice. It's summer vacation, and you're young. You should be having fun."

The girl, Laura, gave him an earnest look.

"Yes, I managed to get some pool time," he relented. "I'll send out an email to the team tomorrow with days and times."

Laura gave a rather loud whoop of joy and darted back to a small gaggle of girls at the other end of the bowling alley, presumably to share the good news.

"What was that about?" I asked, unable to contain my curiosity a moment longer.

"I coach the swim team for a local private school." River ran a finger over my cheek, sending a shiver through me. "Come on, let's bowl. How many more strikes can you get?"

The thought of more strikes was enough to turn my attention back to the game with the ghost of River's touch still lingering.

I'd never met guys who were so comfortable with casual touches, but damn, I enjoyed the attention. The guys were all so sweet.

Glancing around as I took a seat to wait my turn, I noticed Zephyr scowling in my direction.

So, one still remained to be tackled, but I figured I had time to win him over.

CHAPTER SEVEN

ZEPHYR

A sh sank down next to me. "You should make nice with our girl."

I shot him a glare. Did he really not get what my issue was here? How was it that none of them were the slightest bit suspicious?

"I got nothing against her, Ash," I hissed in annoyance, "but something weird is going on. Why the hell did Iunctura happen? No one's ever heard of a fifth. I can't trust her because of that."

"Come on, Zeph, lighten up," he said. "She's sweet. You gotta learn to drop those walls."

Scanning the bowling alley, I frowned when my gaze fell on a guy who kept glancing our way. "What's he staring at us for?"

Ash twisted to take a look and frowned. "That's

Rae's friend, Pierson. He came with her brother to pick Rae up that first night."

"Then why's he staring and not coming over to say hi?" I demanded, my hackles rising at the feeling of being monitored.

Ash crossed his arms over his chest, glanced around, then grinned. "I don't think he's staring at us." He pointed to where a guy who would look at home in any local tattoo and piercing parlor was striding across the lanes from the restrooms. "That's Rae's brother, Devin. They're probably here together, and he was watching for him."

I frowned. "I still don't trust him."

Ash chuckled. "Is there anyone you do trust?"

With an irritated look, I smacked the back of his head. "Yeah, the three of you, moron."

With a wide grin, Ash threw an arm around me and gave my cheek a loud, smacking kiss. "Awe, I love you too, grumpy."

Stupid fuck. I stifled a laugh and shoved Ash. "Go bowl, dweeb."

My eyes roamed while we bowled. Something was off, but I couldn't put a finger on what.

Halfway through the third game, a frisson of wrongness rolled over me like a dark, smothering cloud.

Standing, I rolled my shoulders to rid myself of the sudden tension in them. Whatever this was, it made me restless and more irritated than usual.

I started pacing and shoved at the hair that had fallen into my face. My eyes darted around, trying to find the source of this feeling.

"Zephyr?" Tarin placed a hand on my shoulder. "What's wrong?"

"I don't know." I didn't stop my scan of the alley. "But it's very wrong. I think—"

A stranger sat alone in the last lane. No bowling ball, no game going. He appeared ordinary. Muscular, brown hair, and glasses. But this odd feeling came from him.

I glanced at the guys. "I think it's time to go."

Tarin's gaze found the stranger as well, and he nodded.

I wanted to hustle everyone out right away, but the others insisted on finishing the game. If I protested, I would have seemed insane, but I knew we needed to get the hell away from that guy.

I kept an eye on the guy as we finished up, returned shoes, and paid.

Once we hit the parking lot, the issue of getting home presented itself.

Ash had his bike, and as much as he wanted to take Raegan home, Tarin thought it was a bad idea.

I leaned back against River's Bronco, arms crossed over my chest as I listened to the two of them argue about who would take Raegan home. I didn't care as long as we got the hell out of there.

"Uh, guys?" Raegan called, trying to get their attention. "Ash? Tarin? Guys?"

Oh, for fuck's sake. We needed to go before that guy followed us.

"Shut it, dweebs! The troublemaker is trying to talk!" I hollered.

Silence followed, and the others turned to Raegan with sheepish looks.

"I don't want to be a problem," she said, fiddling with a lock of that odd, stark white hair.

Ash moved next to her, put an arm around her shoulders, and pulled her into a sideways hug. "No, no, baby, not a problem, I swear. Why don't you go with Tarin, huh? Do you have our numbers?"

Her blush couldn't be missed. Neither could Ash's obvious interest in the girl, nor Tarin's. Did they realize they shared that? Could be an issue before long.

She shook her head and held out her cell. "I didn't have it that first night."

The others took her pale pink and gold phone and put in their numbers. When each of their own phones dinged, I knew they sent themselves a text, so they had hers as well.

Ash held the phone out to me, but I shook my head, focused on the front doors of the alley. From the corner of my eye, I noticed him punching something into the phone. A moment later, my phone dinged, alerting me that he added my number.

Whatever. I didn't have any desire to text the troublemaker.

Finished, Ash nudged Raegan's chin and climbed onto his bike as Raegan and Tarin headed toward Tarin's truck.

Halfway there, Raegan stopped and turned back around. "I almost forgot. Mom wants to invite you all over for a thank you barbeque next Saturday."

"We'll be there," Ash called back and glanced pointedly at me. "All of us."

Wonderful.

My gaze shifted from the door to the troublemaker as she climbed into Tarin's truck. I wasn't trying to be an asshole, but something wasn't right about this whole situation. It kept sliding more sideways. River and Ash said I needed to learn to relax, but old habits died hard.

"I don't like this," I grumbled to no one in particular.

"We've noticed," Ash responded.

"That's not what I mean, moron." I watched the taillights of the truck turning out of the parking lot. "I don't like just leaving her like this. Someone tried to kidnap her, and I'm getting some major bad vibes off that guy inside. We still don't have any answers about why the Iunctura happened, or what exactly she is, or why the hell someone would want to kidnap her."

Everything that had happened since that troublemaker showed up in our house bothered me. Something big was going on, and she was at the center, even if she didn't know it.

I blew out a breath and looked up at the sky.

A few stars twinkled merrily as some dark, wispy clouds floated along. I closed my eyes as a light breeze caressed my face. Turning into the breeze, I slowed my breathing and let the wind talk.

According to the tutors I'd had when I'd first met the others, it wasn't actually possible to hear the wind talk because the wind didn't talk. I knew what I heard, though, what I felt when I blocked everything else out. So, I listened and heard the warning it carried to me.

"I don't think we should leave her alone." I knew we shouldn't. The wind said as much.

When I opened my eyes, Ash and River met mine, their own filled with concern.

Sometimes I found myself flabbergasted at how much they trusted me.

"Maybe we should set a watch up at her house," Ash suggested. "I still haven't heard back from Dad, so I have no idea what we should do. I'll try to call him."

Ash gnawed on his bottom lip as he stared at the end of the parking lot like he could wish Tarin back.

I didn't blame him.

"We have to be careful," I warned them. "Our world can be a bit much to take when you aren't born into it."

Unlike Ash, Tarin, and River, I didn't grow up knowing the world I now inhabited. It was a shock and a relief when I discovered exactly what was up with me. How would the naïve little troublemaker deal with it?

River spoke for the first time since Tarin and Raegan left. "Well, I was going to head out to the beach tomorrow, but I can take a watch tonight and go another day."

Before River even finished or I could say

anything, Ash shook his head. "Don't do that. You don't get out to the beach too often. I'll take tonight, then tomorrow morning we can work out a schedule with Tarin. Damn, but this would be easier if she lived with us. At least, we aren't skirting around her parents."

I grabbed Ash around the neck, pulling him in and giving him a sideways hug. "Be careful. Something doesn't feel right."

Part of me wanted to go with him, felt like he shouldn't be alone tonight, but I had a business to run and early mornings tended to be a part of it.

Ash laughed and shoved away. "I'll be fine. See you in the morning."

And with that, Ash pulled on his helmet and tore out of the parking lot.

Worry gnawed at my gut as River and I headed home.

⚓⚓⚓

Despite nothing happening on Ash's watch, the worry and feeling of something being off only increased in the days leading up to the barbecue. It hung like a shroud over the house, at least to me. The wind carried its warning every time I listened.

I might have issues with the oddity of the things happening, but it didn't mean I wanted harm to come to the troublemaker. It made me a grumpier shit than usual.

Tarin tried to get me to talk, thinking I might be suppressing things.

Ash tried to get me to go clubbing to forget about it.

Even River tried asking me to meditate.

Nothing helped though, especially not when the warning carried on the wind got stronger.

Saturday came long before I wanted to face it. The idea of a family barbeque sent frissons of trepidation crawling down my spine. What the hell did one do at a family barbeque? How did one dress for a family barbecue? I didn't have any experience with families outside my Genus.

Staring into my perfectly ordered closet, I growled and grabbed a pair of khaki cargo shorts. I was overthinking this.

After slipping into the shorts, I grabbed a white ribbed tank out of the drawer and threw it on first, before pulling on a short-sleeved button-down with pale blue, green, and white swirls, leaving it open. Sliding on my sandals, I joined the others downstairs, noticing they were dressed in much the same fashion.

The guys yammered as we drove, but I didn't participate. Instead, I let my thoughts drift.

Too many odd things kept happening. That one thought stuck in my head on repeat. I wanted answers, but I couldn't even figure out what the right questions were. Even if we knew where to look, it would take years to go through the information at the Tabularium, and I had a feeling that wasn't where our answers would be found.

We needed the Sages, but Ash's dad, Michael, was right when he said they were hard to contact. As the heads of our world, the Concilium Sapientes were often on the road. They were also the best source of information. Things, stories, and information were passed down only from one Sage to another. Things one wouldn't find at the Tabularium.

My mind drifted back to the troublemaker and this barbeque, but I didn't want to think about that. Family was a foreign concept.

A hand suddenly clasped my own and squeezed.

I glanced over to see River smiling at me.

"You'll be okay. No worries." River squeezed my hand again, then went back to talking to Ash and Tarin.

I shook my head. Somehow, Tarin always knew when I needed to be brought out of my thoughts.

A few minutes later, we pulled into Raegan's driveway and parked.

The man who answered had short, messy, dirty blond hair, light blue eyes, a light beard, and a wide smile. "You must be the boys responsible for my baby girl's safety." A laugh escaped as he spoke. "Well, come in. We're all out back, and I just fired up the grill. I'm Troy, by the way."

We walked into a decent size yard with stone pavers laid tightly together to form a deck. A covered seating area held comfortable-looking chairs and couches circled around a brick fire pit, and a large, white, glass-topped outdoor dining set waited to one side. White twinkle lights were strung from a wooden canopy and wound around the support poles.

A short distance to one side, a large charcoal grill and smoker butted up against a long, slate-topped counter with a sink. Smoke curled into the air from the open chimney on the grill, gray tendrils following the flow of the wind currents long after it appeared to dissipate.

For a moment, I wanted to join them, to ride away with the tendrils of smoke, but I shook the feeling off.

The low hum and beat of music drifted into the air from hidden speakers.

Homemade PVC soccer goals were set up in the grass, and Pierson shot goals into one, the troublemaker doing her best to block them but failing miserably. As I watched, Pierson shot the ball. It flew well above the troublemaker's reach, hitting the upper left corner of the goal.

She stuck her bottom lip out and stomped a foot while glaring at Pierson.

He laughed at her antics.

I couldn't help my own chuckle when the troublemaker marched over to where the ball rested in the net, her knees lifting high and her feet coming down in big, over-exaggerated stomps. She snatched up the ball and resumed her starting position, arms wrapped around the ball. She cocked her head and stuck her tongue out at a still-laughing Pierson.

Their antics held me enthralled, an odd pang worming its way into my gut as I continued to watch.

Pierson pointed a threatening finger at the troublemaker with narrowed eyes, and she shook her head, her white ponytail swinging wildly. Pierson took a couple steps toward her, and she stepped back, head still shaking. A step forward, another step back. One more step forward, and Raegan took off, the ball still clutched in her arms.

She didn't stand a chance as Pierson chased after,

catching her around the waist and lifting her off her feet as she scream-laughed.

Pierson grabbed the ball with one hand, then put the troublemaker back on her feet. He ran a hand through his hair, shaking it so droplets of sweat flew off.

She shoved him and turned toward the patio area, her eyes lighting up when they fell on us.

My stomach twisted. I didn't know why, but I didn't like the sensation at all. Scowling, I stormed over to the nearest chair and threw myself down.

The troublemaker flung herself at Ash, who caught her and hugged her tight before setting her back on her feet. She gave quick hugs to Tarin and River, then looked around, finally spotting me.

I groaned quietly and deepened my scowl when she headed in my direction. She might be innocent, but I wasn't ready to trust her or welcome her into our world, our lives. We'd only known her a couple weeks, after all. It took the better part of a year to let River, Tarin, and Ash in, even after I knew who I was, and we were living and training together.

My scowl didn't work to drive her off. Instead, the troublemaker sank down next to me. She didn't try to touch me or hug me. She simply folded her hands in her lap and smiled warmly. "Hello, Z. I'm glad you came."

Z? What the—? My face scrunched at the unfamiliar nickname.

Despite trying to clear the expression quickly, the troublemaker didn't miss it. She pulled her bottom lip into her mouth with her teeth.

Oh, for fuck's sake.

With a sigh, I reached over and dragged her lip out of her mouth with a finger. "Don't do that. Drives me nuts."

"Sorry," she mumbled. "You don't like me calling you Z? Zephyr's just kind of a mouthful."

She gave a half-hearted shrug and stared at her hands, still clasped in her lap.

It took everything in me not to roll my eyes. "I don't care what you call me. Never had a nickname before, that's all."

"Oh." She cocked her head to the side. "You've never had a nickname? But didn't your parents…"

Not ready to go there with her, I got up and walked off, putting some much-needed distance between us. I knew she meant well, but not here, not yet.

From the corner of my eye, I noticed River join

her and moved just close enough to hear their whispered words.

"I don't understand. All I did was ask if his parents ever called him anything but Zephyr." Hurt laced her voice.

I swore I could hear the tears threatening, but I froze at the idea of trying to fix it.

"Zephyr's life growing up was complicated," River explained. "Let's just say that his mother had other priorities than her son."

Thanks a fucking lot, River. If I'd wanted her to know that, I'd have fucking told her! So much for not here, not yet.

"Oh my gosh. I had no idea." Her eyes widened in horror. "I should apologize."

"No! Don't do that." River held his hands up to stop her. "Just leave him be. He'll be back to grumpy old Zephyr in no time."

I didn't need to hear the rest of the conversation, so I wandered around the backyard, stopping every now and then to listen to the wind or watch Pierson's fancy footwork with the soccer ball.

Pierson must have felt my stare because he suddenly looked up.

Our eyes met, his holding a hundred questions.

I stepped forward, intending to go talk to the kid and figure out what was bothering me about the guy.

A pop sounded under my foot, like plastic cracking or breaking. I looked down right in time to catch a huge, harsh spray of water straight in the face, the stream soaking me.

I sputtered and swatted at the water even as I backed out of the spray.

A couple shouts sounded, and a hand belonging to Troy clamped down on my shoulder. "Hey, you okay there?"

I didn't want to appear rude, but I couldn't help being intensely uncomfortable with the man touching me. I moved out from under his hand. "Yeah, fine. I'll just go find a bathroom and dry off."

"Upstairs, second door on the left," he directed.

As I stepped into the kitchen, I looked around. The place was odd. Papers were scattered across the countertops, and a few dirty dishes sat in the sink. In the living room, a couple throw pillows haphazardly decorated the couch, and little knick-knacks and souvenirs cluttered shelves. And there were framed photos everywhere. Pictures of Devin and Raegan at various ages. Pictures of family vacations and holidays.

It was odd to see the trappings of a family's past

displayed so prominently. Was this kind of thing normal, as opposed to the near-sterile places I grew up in?

I found the bathroom easily enough, as it was one of only two open doors, and the other was farther down. More pictures decorated the beige walls of the hall. The door directly across from the bathroom featured a vibrant blue, green, and purple flower emblazoned with the troublemaker's name. So much decoration and homeyness. It felt strange.

Dismissing the feeling, I entered the bathroom.

Grabbing the fluffy white towel hanging from the silver towel bar, I ran it over my face and hair but didn't bother with my clothes. I'd dry fast enough outside.

As I hung up the towel, I caught movement out of the corner of my eye and turned my head, wondering who followed me up.

But no one waited at the doorway for me to leave the bathroom.

Not one to let something like that go, I crept to the bathroom door and peered around the frame.

What the hell?

A short distance down the hall, Pierson tiptoed on silent feet to a door that was cracked open. He leaned against the wall next to it, peered into the crack, then sighed.

Seriously, what the fuck?

Pierson's eyes lingered on the cracked door as he pushed off from the wall and backed away, coming toward the bathroom once more.

I quickly ducked back inside, stepped behind the door, and waited several minutes to be sure Pierson left before I stepped out into the hall. Curious, I glanced toward the cracked door, wondering what Pierson had been looking at. That had easily been the oddest, most suspicious thing I'd seen Pierson do yet.

But it wasn't my house, and it wasn't my problem, so I headed back downstairs.

"Hey, man, that sprinkler got you good," called out an unfamiliar voice.

Glancing up, I spotted Devin leaning on the kitchen counter.

Okay? I figured Pierson had to be looking at Devin's room since I knew the troublemaker's room was across the hall from the bathroom. If Devin wasn't in the room, what had Pierson been looking at?

He held up the bottle of beer in his hand. "You look like you could use one of these."

I could definitely use a beer. Cracking a small smile, I chuckled and nodded.

Devin grabbed a couple more beers out of the fridge, handed me one, then headed into the backyard. "Come on, before Mom hunts us down for being antisocial."

I followed him back out and took up residence in the seat I'd vacated earlier, sipping the beer and watching the others as they hung out. The atmosphere was very relaxed, and for a moment, I wished I could enjoy the easy camaraderie of the others.

I didn't know how to handle parents, though, especially not the kind of parents Raegan had. Her folks laughed and bantered with her, Devin, and even Pierson, giving as good as they got when teased. They were very touchy people as well, and I didn't do touching well. I didn't like people I didn't know touching me, only barely tolerating handshakes. Yet, every time I stood, Raegan's mom hugged me, or her dad slapped my back or rested a hand on my shoulder.

I tried to stay on the fringes as much as possible.

When my stomach began to gnaw on my backbone, I grabbed a plate of the food that had been laid out on the counter near the grill.

Troy grinned when I found myself next to him. "Hey, hey! Look, I know you guys don't think you did anything, but seriously, thank you. My baby girl means the world to me, and there aren't many that would have taken time to help her."

My eyes widened as I stared a beat too long at the man. What was I supposed to say to that? I wasn't even there when Ash rescued Raegan, and I'd snarled at her at the house.

I jumped when a hand clamped down on my shoulder.

"Really, sir," Ash's voice came from behind me. "It was no big deal. Honestly, she got herself out of that trunk. I wouldn't have even known she was in there."

Seeing an opportunity, I grabbed my plate and made myself scarce.

I hated my social awkwardness. I hadn't exactly been allowed to socialize much as a kid. Most of the time, my mother, or whatever pimp, john, or *boyfriend* she was with at the time, was happy to shove me in a room and ignore my existence.

Shaking off the morose thoughts, I noticed the troublemaker strolling toward me.

She grinned, her smile puffing out her cheeks and lifting her eyes. She pointed at my empty plate. "Are you enjoying it?"

I nodded. No need to be impolite.

"Good."

An awkward silence fell until the strains of something slow and soft drifted from the hidden speakers. The girl turned her head, and when I followed her gaze, I noticed her parents dancing on the patio. When I turned back, she beamed up at me expectantly.

"Hey, baby." Ash strolled up to us and wrapped an arm around the troublemaker. "Dance?"

Her smile could have lit up the night as Ash spun her into a dance, and I breathed a sigh of relief.

CHAPTER EIGHT

ASH

Bored, I leaned back against the huge alder tree near the edge of Rae's property. The dark night hung around me, providing nice shadows to hide in.

While Rae's parents knew we watched the house at night, they'd asked us to stay out of sight. They didn't want to upset their daughter.

Nights like these, heavy and still, made me restless. Usually, I headed into Seattle to the clubs. While the others didn't like it, they knew I needed it, needed the drinks, the hint of danger, the possibility of a warm body pressed against mine as we danced. I never took those girls home, never slept with them. I wasn't stupid. But the flirting and dancing eased something inside me.

Clubs weren't an option tonight. There weren't many options when I was on watch.

With a snap of my fingers, a small flame sparked to life. The bright red-orange flame danced on the edge of my thumb, flickering in the light breeze. With a twist of my hand, the little flame danced and rolled, the way someone else might with a ball.

Handling a small flame this way was one of the first things I'd learned at Illustratio Academy when my element manifested at eight. As a child, I found it fascinating and could spend hours experimenting.

Now, though, I got bored in minutes.

Frustrated, I flung the tiny flame. A few feet away, the grass caught and flared brightly for a half second before I snuffed the fire.

I glanced up at the window I'd decided was Rae's. The barbeque a few nights before was fun, but we were no closer to revealing ourselves to Rae, which frustrated the hell out of me. We were moving so damn slow. It felt wrong. We needed to figure out what her element was, train her to use it, and help her learn to protect herself.

Fuck it. I needed to walk. I shot off a hopeful text.

Ash: you up?

The response came immediately.

Raegan: Yes. Can't sleep. You either, huh?

Ash: No. Happens a lot. I get restless at night. Interested in joining me for a walk? I promise to keep you safe from all the dangerous car trunks.

Raegan: Hell, yeah! See you in 15?

Ash: Meet you by the tree in your yard.

She didn't text back, but precisely fifteen minutes later, her white hair flew out from behind her as she dashed across the lawn.

Flinging herself at me, she hugged me tight around the neck.

I squeezed her back, then set her away from me. No need for her to know exactly how much I enjoyed her curvy body against mine.

She vibrated with excitement.

"Ready for a walk?" I held a hand out.

She hesitated for a half beat, grabbed it, and laced our fingers together.

I ran a hand through my blond-tipped spikes and looked around as we headed down the street, guilt spearing my gut. We were supposed to watch the house, and she wasn't supposed to know.

She didn't know, though.

Since she gave me so much time before she came out, she obviously thought I texted her from my house. And really, the point of watching the house was to keep her safe. What better way to keep her safe than to be with her?

Sure, I was splitting hairs, but it was after midnight, so to hell with it. It all sounded reasonable.

We walked in silence for the first several minutes, which helped the restlessness, but now that I was alone with Raegan, I wanted, no *needed*, to know more about her. She fascinated me from the second she'd landed on my feet, and it had nothing to do with the Iunctura.

"So, did you use a whole bottle of bleach to get your hair that white?" It might be odd, but I wondered the most about her hair color.

"No bleach." Laughter laced her voice. "My hair is naturally this color. I used to hate it when I was little because I'd get teased all the time. My mom tried to dye it once, but dye doesn't work on my hair, apparently."

Reaching over, I brushed a stray strand from the side of her face. "Well, it's beautiful, and it suits you."

Even in the dim light thrown by the occasional streetlight, I noticed her blush. Silence fell again, comfortable and easy, as we strolled along hand-in-hand.

I wanted to ask more, but I couldn't pick the questions apart in my head. Time seemed to stop around us, and all of my original intentions drifted away in the breeze. Having Rae here soothed the restlessness I'd been feeling more and more lately, if it was even that. I didn't need the noise, the beat, the rush, that I normally craved. It was enough to just hold her hand.

Fingers ran over my arm and traced the tattoo there.

A little shiver ran up my spine at her soft touch.

We stopped under a streetlight, so I took the opportunity to take in all her cuteness again. The light illuminated her face. Delicate, with a light smattering of freckles across her cheeks and nose. Long eyelashes, framing pale gray eyes. Everything from her stark white hair to her pale skin was light and airy. She was no stick, which I liked a lot. Some would think her near-colorless appearance strange or off-putting, but I thought her a beautiful fantasy come to life.

"Did you leave it just an outline on purpose?" Her question broke through my internal ramblings.

I shook my head, both in answer to her question and to clear my thoughts. The second wasn't as effective as I'd hoped. "It was meant to be colored, but the artist moved before it was finished."

Her fingers continued to move over my arm, the

soft touch shutting my brain down as she stroked up my shoulder and over my neck. Her finger ran across my ear lobe and the crystal stud there.

A slight tremble ran through her, a soft, dreamy expression taking over her face as though she was lost in the moment.

My breath caught in my throat as I fought to keep her from seeing the way she was driving me crazy. I should grab her hand, push her away. She was too innocent to know her touch sent shockwaves through me. I should have stopped her when her fingers moved across my cheek and began playing with the hoop in my eyebrow. That was what I should have done, but I didn't. Instead, I closed my eyes and breathed in her clean, crisp scent as I leaned into her touch.

Thank the mother our emotions rarely had much of an effect on our powers because, otherwise, I'd have sent the nearest house up in flames.

Her fingers ran over my closed eyes, down my other cheek, and stroked across my neck. She traced the edge of the flame tattoo that peeked out from under my shirt. I couldn't stop my body from reacting, and my hands moved to rest on the swell of her hips, pulling her against me.

"So many needles to your skin." Her voice was

soft, curious and did nothing to help stop the heat flowing through me. "You must enjoy the rush."

I needed to break the moment, to stop the desires, the need suddenly raging through me. I stepped back, pulled the red, sleeveless shirt over my head, and turned so my back faced her.

A quiet gasp was all the warning I received before her fingers returned to my neck.

Fuck. Not what I intended. Not the best idea, either.

The heat of her body mere inches from my own sent blood racing south. My eyes closed as she stroked my back, following the path the flames made as they ran down to my hip.

She seemed to follow every mark, every line. "Such incredible work. So detailed."

The words wormed into my ear but failed to really register.

I'd hoped that turning away from her would break her hold over me. Instead, it seemed like everything heightened. Her soft touches, the heat of her nearness, and her breath on my bare skin all worked to drive me out of my mind.

I clenched my fists at my side, fighting for control that rapidly slipped away. My body trembled as she admired the art on my skin. I told myself to pull away from her touch, but my body refused to respond. We'd barely had a chance to get to know her, after all, and there was so much we still hid.

Desperate, I flung my fingers out, sending a spurt of flame into the ground in front of me and praying Rae didn't notice. It didn't help the heat inside. I flung out another, hoping to calm the fire racing through me.

Nothing. No relief.

My gaze found the scorch marks and widened when I noticed they formed a lopsided heart on the concrete.

Her finger found my neck again, and she circled back around to my front while I suppressed a whimper.

"It's really some amazing art. It almost seems alive." Her eyes caught mine, and I found myself drowning in them.

What the hell was happening? What was she doing to me? There was a pull on the Iunctura, more intense, more insistent than anything I'd ever experienced. I couldn't resist anymore, couldn't stop myself. With a groan, I gave in.

Grasping her waist, I pulled her against me, leaned down, and captured her mouth. She stilled, but only for a second before whimpering and melting into the kiss. Her arms snaked up to wrap around my neck.

I kept the kiss soft and sweet until she parted her lips with a small whimper. I nibbled at her lower lip, and she gasped. Wasting no time, I dove into her mouth, the bar in my tongue stroking against her as we tangled together. Her grip tightened, and she pressed against me. My hands found the edge of her shirt, worked their way inside, and stroked over the bare skin of her back and belly.

Elements, she tasted sweet. It wasn't until she squirmed against me, and a car honked at us that my brain clicked back on, and I realized how close to the edge I was.

I took a couple quick steps backward, out of her reach, panting softly as I tried to pull myself together. She stood, illuminated like a spotlight by the lamp, face flushed, eyes glazed, lips swollen, hair mussed, panting softly. I groaned and fought the urge to yank her back against me and keep going. I wanted to drown in her, and that thought yanked me firmly back to reality.

"C'mon." My voice sounded flat as I ran a hand through my hair. "Let's get you home. It's late."

Turning, I headed back the way we came, keeping

my hands tucked deep into my pockets so I wouldn't reach for her again.

Silence hung between us once more. Not awkward, but certainly not the comfortable, easy silence from before.

Halfway back to her place, slender fingers tugged my hand from its pocket and laced through my own.

When I glanced at her, a smile played on Rae's lips, though her eyes remained firmly staring straight ahead.

I ran a thumb across the back of her hand, and a small, desperate whimper escaped her.

Returning my gaze to the sidewalk, I smiled, pleased that I hadn't been the only one on the verge of coming apart.

CHAPTER NINE

RIVER

"Riva! Riva! Lookie me!"

I looked up from my phone to find Bethany spinning in circles, her little blond head thrown back and her arms held out from her sides. Watching her spin, pure delight on her face, warmed my heart. I didn't get to see enough of her. She was growing up so fast, and I missed so much since I moved out.

"Baby girl, you're going to fall down if you keep that up. Please be careful."

"Then I be a bridge!" She squealed as she quit spinning and ran over to me.

I'd brought her to the park since it was such a beautiful day, and I knew how much she loved it.

She threw herself into my lap, giggling.

"A bridge?" I asked, curious to see where this was going. Her mind worked in unique ways.

Wrapping my arms around her, I hugged her tight and breathed in her sweet baby scent. Who knew three-year-olds smelled so good? Of course, I might be a bit biased, or it might be the lotion I'd put on her earlier.

"Uh-huh. I be a London bridge fall down," as she said that, she collapsed across my lap, dissolving into giggles.

"You know, I don't think bridges giggle so much." I danced my fingers over her belly, making her squeal and screech until I sat her up. "C'mon, baby girl. You better finish eating, or momma will kill me."

Bethany plopped down on the blanket we'd spread out and popped a grape into her mouth. She was such a sweet little girl. Sometimes, I wished I didn't work so much. I might get to see her more if I didn't, but she was precisely the reason I did.

"River!"

Glancing up, I spotted a familiar face headed toward us.

With a grin, I stood.

"Hey, Mom." Leaning over, I kissed her cheek, then stood back to assess her appearance.

Serena Sage was a stunning woman, with her light

brown hair pulled back away from her face and wearing a pair of scrubs with ice cream cone people on them. Her blue eyes held dark circles, and I wondered if she'd been working overtime again. She worked at a local pediatrician's office, so she could be home at night with Bethany, but occasionally, the clinic ran long.

Bethany squealed when she spotted her. "Momma!" she cried out and jumped up to hug Mom's legs.

Mom picked her up, nuzzled her, and set her back down. "Was she good today?"

"Yeah, Mom. She's always good."

We both watched Bethany as she ate and danced around.

"She looks so much like Hugh these days." The thought escaped before I could suppress it.

Grief crossed Mom's face, making me wish I could take the words back. I knew how painful it still was, even almost four years after he died. My stepdad had never seen his daughter, had never even known about her.

"Come on, Bethie," she called. "Time to go home."

Together, Mom and I made short work of packing things away, gathering up the blanket and Bethany's toys. I tucked the containers with the food into the cooler I'd brought.

"Do you need anything, Mom?" I asked as I hugged her and Bethany. Mom shook her head. "Are you sure? You know you only need to ask."

"I'm sure, River." Mom laughed. "Don't you have some nice girl to spend your money on?"

For a second, Raegan flashed into my mind before I dismissed it. I barely knew her. I did know my mom, though, and I'd tucked some money into Bethany's bag for her. With luck, by the time she found it, she would assume she'd tucked it away.

"No."

"It's 'cause you work too much." She shook her head and kissed my cheek. "Bye, sweetheart."

Bethany waved and blew me a kiss. "Bye, Riva!"

"Bye, Bethie. Bye, Mom." I watched as they headed back to Mom's car and plotted what to do the next time I took care of Bethany.

I loved my little sister, and I tried to take care of her as often as I could so Mom could get things done or go out. Not that she went out often.

When I bent to grab my stuff, a flash of white hair made me freeze and straighten. My gaze met a pale silver one, and I smiled as Raegan waved.

She dashed over, grinning wide.

"Hey." Her voice came out a bit breathless, sending a jolt of delight through me.

It took me by surprise since I had spent little time with her and didn't feel as connected to her as Ash or even Tarin seemed to be. The wind blew her hair around, sending stray strands into her face as she beamed up at me. She made a futile effort to push a few back.

"Hey, what are you doing here?" I asked.

"Just hanging out." Rae shifted her weight, bouncing slightly on her toes. "I think Pierson and I were driving Mom nuts because she shoved the keys into Devin's hands and told him to find a lake to drop us in." She laughed, the tinkling sound sending another jolt of delight through me.

Glancing around, I didn't see either of the guys. "So, where are Devin and Pierson, then?"

"Devin's over there." Raegan pointed to where Devin sat on a nearby picnic table, a busty brunette clinging to him. A couple other girls sat with him, and I could swear that cartoon hearts were coming out of their eyes. "And Pier took off. He's not big on crowds."

"So, you got left on your own?"

She nodded.

For some reason, the idea that her friends abandoned her bothered me. We still didn't know why or who had tried to kidnap her, or who the weird guy at the bowling alley had been.

Hell, we'd barely had time to dig into it.

Zephyr could still hear the warning of danger for Raegan on the wind, and a couple nights ago, Tarin had sworn he'd seen someone sneaking around in her backyard. Had both Devin and Pierson just dismissed all of that so easily to leave her on her own? Even if they didn't think of any of that as serious, there were still dangers that could befall a beautiful young woman on her own. Why would they take a chance like that?

Rae shrugged. "It's not a big thing."

I reminded myself that she didn't know all the things we did. Of course, neither did Devin or Pierson or, heck, even her folks. Since I did, though, I wasn't about to leave her on her own. Not to mention this would be a chance to get to know her a bit.

Her gaze darted back to Devin, and she frowned. Her shoulders fell, and she shook her head. I didn't know what caused the sadness leaking from every line of her body, but right then, I needed to fix it.

"Take your shoes off." I stepped out of my

sandals. When Rae's nose scrunched up and confusion crossed her face, I added, "Trust me?"

Eyes wide, bent to take off her shoes and placed them next to mine.

Slipping my hand into hers, I laced our fingers together and led her down to where the lake lapped at the shore, gently rolling the waters onto the sand. No one would notice her here.

I turned her so we faced each other.

She shot me a quizzical smile.

"Close your eyes," I instructed, and she complied.

The trust she showed right now warmed me. I grasped her other hand and closed my eyes. Reaching out with my power, I grabbed the water lapping at our ankles. I sent it into tiny, individual whirlpools around each of Rae's ankles, then joined the streams. It wasn't necessary to close my eyes for this, but manipulating elements required concentration. Nature was fickle and didn't exactly want to listen to anyone.

Opening my eyes, I checked that everything worked the way I wanted, then leaned down to whisper in her ear. "Open your eyes and look at your feet."

When she did, she gasped. Her smile widened, and she stared at the water swirling around her ankles with wonder and delight. The flowing water formed an infinity symbol around her ankles.

"How?" I heard the reverence in her voice.

"Magic," I whispered to her.

She laughed and smacked my arm. Concentration broken, the water returned to its natural path. I barely noticed, too busy getting lost in the twinkling laughter in Raegan's eyes. When a shudder traveled through her, it pulled me back to reality. Cold water chilled my ankles, which must be what caused her to shiver, so we headed back to where we'd left our shoes.

As Rae sank to the grass, her gaze fell on my guitar case.

"Do you play?" She tilted her head toward the case, then cringed and shook her head. "Stupid question. You wouldn't have a guitar if you didn't. Sorry."

Not wanting to bring attention to her embarrassment by commenting on it, I instead said, "Bethany, my little sister, loves music and dancing. We were hanging out today while my mom was at work, so I brought it with us to play for her."

"Would you play for me?" The red in her cheeks deepened.

I liked the idea of playing for her. The only other

time I'd felt a pull this strong had been when I'd met Zephyr. I checked to be sure Devin wasn't looking for her.

He still held court on the same picnic table, but he glanced our way and waved.

Grabbing the case, I pulled out the simple acoustic guitar, then settled on the grass, facing Rae, and fiddled with tuning the strings. It didn't really need to be tuned, but I used the time to figure out what to play.

I finally chose one of my favorite country songs. As I reached the first chorus, I lifted my gaze to look at her and nearly lost the song entirely. She'd settled on the grass, legs tucked under her, fingers idly stroking the ground, and her beautiful silver eyes fixed on me. The setting sun framed her in pinks and purples. She stole my breath, and she didn't even know it. I couldn't tear my eyes away from her. She swayed in place to the music, a dreamy smile gracing her face. The last note of the song rang out and hung suspended in time between us.

Then, she was being dragged to her feet.

"Come on." Pierson held firmly to her arm. "We gotta go." His eyes flicked to me. "Later, River."

And with that, he pulled Raegan off toward Devin.

When they neared him, Devin hopped off the table, ignoring the girls who clamored for him to stay, and the trio left me with my own thoughts.

CHAPTER TEN

RAEGAN

A shining sun, a fresh paycheck, and restlessness made Devin want to head to the Outlets, and of course, he dragged me, so I dragged Pierson. Devin wanted to head to the leather store first.

With a sigh, I wrapped my arms around my middle and ducked my head, so my hair fell into my face. Through the veil of hair, I spied Pierson shooting me a confused look, but I wasn't ready to talk about things. I kind of wanted to go back to my room and wallow in confusion for a while.

Devin glanced back, a frown crossing his face as he took me in.

Closing the short distance, he flung an arm around my shoulder and pulled me in for a hug without a word. I loved that my brother knew when words were needed and when they weren't. I couldn't handle words right now, but the gentle hug did a lot to calm my mind.

With his arm still around me, we headed into the store while Pierson held the door.

I didn't hide the smile when Devin bee-lined for the rack of jackets.

"Really? Jackets? In the middle of summer?" Disbelief laced Pierson's voice.

"Should always be prepared. Besides, some people find leather jackets sexy." Devin shot him a grin and removed his arm from around me to grab one of the jackets off the rack and slip it on. "What do you think, Pierson?"

Pierson froze.

I swore those two were going to kill me before they figured shit out.

Moving to his side, I grabbed Pier's hand and squeezed. He squeezed back, then tugged me behind him to another section of the store without answering Devin's question.

Devin's laugh followed us.

I kept an eye on them as we browsed, amused by their interactions, letting them take my mind off things. Every so often Devin would find us with another jacket in hand, slip it on, and ask for Pierson's opinion. Never mind. He couldn't be more obvious if he tried. Not that Pier noticed. Pierson never said anything, just froze for half a second before tugging me off to some other section of the store. I didn't even try to hide the giggles when we started revisiting sections.

"What are you doing, Pier?" I asked through my laughter.

"Trying to stay away from your brother." He pouted, actually pouted! I didn't know whether to comfort him or giggle more. "Why does he insist on asking my opinion on every fuckin' jacket in the place?"

"Maybe he just wants to be sure he looks okay. I mean, isn't that why you ask for opinions?" I attempted to sound reasonable, but my giggles probably weren't helping.

"He's not asking for yours," Pierson said, still pouting as he dragged us off again.

I glanced around to find Devin heading our way once more.

"Maybe because I'm his sister, and I don't care what he looks like." I tried to sound reasonable and failed miserably.

"Will you stop laughing at me?" he demanded.

I took a couple of gulping breaths to choke back my laughter. "If you stop acting like you're two! He just wants another opinion, Pierson. What's wrong with that?"

I didn't think he intended for me to hear his muttered, "Everything."

As he said it, I spotted Devin getting closer, so I gripped Pierson's hand to keep him from bolting.

"Just tell him what you think, for crying out loud!" I hissed as Pierson stilled.

Devin stopped a couple feet away and smiled at Pierson. "What do you think of this one?"

Honestly, I thought it was the best of the bunch, but mine wasn't the opinion Devin wanted.

I glanced at Pierson just in time to see him swallow hard. His hold on my hand turned into a death grip, but his voice came out steady. "Yeah, that's the best one yet."

"Sweet." Devin looked smug as he turned away. "I'll check out and meet you guys outside, okay?"

While my brother made his purchase, Pierson tugged me out of the store like Cerberus was on our heels.

Outside, he took a deep gulp of air with his eyes closed, looking remarkably like a man who'd escaped a death sentence or something.

I wanted to laugh until I caught sight of the fountain nearby, and my earlier worries slammed back into my brain.

As Devin rejoined us, I pulled my hand from Pierson's.

He shot me a questioning look.

I smiled to reassure him and tucked my hands into my shorts, my fingers skimming my phone. As the boys headed off, I pulled my phone out and scrolled through the series of texts from last night, the ones that sent me tumbling into my own head.

"Rae?" Fingers snapped in my face.

My head jerked up, hair falling into my face, and suppressed the nasty words on the tip of my tongue. I hated when people did that.

Pierson brushed back my bangs, worry lacing his own. "You okay?"

"Yeah, I'm fine." I shot him a smile that must have eased his worry, because he guided me into another store behind Devin.

It wasn't until we were inside that I realized they pulled me into the chocolate store. Even the appearance and temptation of all the delicious chocolate goodness didn't pull me from my funk.

Standing in the middle of the store, phone in hand, I flipped through my recent pictures. I stopped on one, my finger skimming over a picture of Ash that I took at the barbecue. I still remembered the heat of his lips on mine and the startling feel of his tongue piercing. I'd never been kissed like that, and the memory still made my pulse quicken.

Another swipe revealed a picture of River, and I remember that moment standing in the water. I had felt a connection with him and imagined what it would be like to kiss him, too.

What was I doing?

Annoyed, I shoved the damn phone back into my pocket. It didn't do anything to help, though. Closing my eyes, I tried to let the smell of chocolate chase away my worries. Instead, annoyed, sea-green eyes floated in my mind, only to be replaced by a pair of warm, golden ones, emotions flashing wildly in them.

My breaths shortened, my throat trying to close.

When a hand squeezed my shoulder, my eyes flew open to find Pierson standing in front of me.

"That's it. Something's wrong. Come on." Pierson slid his arm around my shoulder and steered me out, calling over his shoulder, "Devin, we're going out by the fountain."

"Okay." He held up a basket of candy. "I'll just pay for these and meet you out there."

Pierson paused us at the door. "Actually, can you

head over to the sub shop and grab us some lunch first?"

"Yeah, sure." Devin didn't need to ask what we wanted. We'd been to enough sub shops to have each other's favorite sandwiches memorized.

While Devin had his own friends, college buddies and people from the tattoo parlor he worked at, over the last several months, he'd been spending more and more time with Pierson and me. I didn't mind. We'd always been pretty close, and I'd worried we'd lose that when we moved here. I'd thought he might move out as soon as we were settled. Thankfully, he'd opted to stay while finishing out college.

Pierson pushed on my shoulder, making me sit down hard on the stone edge of the fountain. He plopped down next to me, pulled his knees up, and turned my way, crossing his legs on the edge of the fountain.

"Spill," he commanded. "What is going on with you today?"

I didn't know if I was ready to talk, but Pierson would push until he had answers.

Sighing, I handed over my phone after bringing up the messages from last night. I knew what they said. I'd memorized them.

Tarin: What's up, Sunshine?

Raegan: Did you just call me Sunshine?

Tarin: Yeah. Your name shortened is Rae, so I called you Sunshine. Like a Rae of Sunshine. You hate it, don't you?

Raegan: No, no. I love it. Promise. :)

Tarin: Are you going to the shelter tomorrow?

Raegan: No, I usually go on Saturdays while Pierson is at soccer. Makes it easier for Devin since he gives us both rides and they are close together.

Tarin: I can give you a ride whenever I'm going, if you want.

Raegan: I'll think about it. Thanks for the offer. It would be nice to go more.

Tarin: Sweet, I'll let you know when I'm going, but until then, how about a movie and dinner Friday?

Raegan: Um. Okay. Sure.

Tarin: Great! See you then. Night, Sunshine.

Raegan: Night.

Pierson gave a small smile as he finished reading.

I didn't let him say anything. Instead, I took the phone and opened a second set of texts before I handed it back.

Pierson's eyes widened, but he dutifully read.

River: You ever been surfing?

Raegan: No.

River: You're kidding, right? Didn't you live like twenty minutes from the beach?

Raegan: Embarrassing, I know. I've done the one with the little board you lay on. Bodyboarding, I think?

River: That does not count.

Raegan: I kind of got flipped by a really big wave and swallowed a ton of water. Scared the heck out of me.

River: How old were you?

Raegan: 7

River: Okay, seriously. That doesn't count for anything.

Raegan: :P

River: Don't stick it out unless you plan to use it. On my days off, I like to try to get out. You could join me next time. Get you on a board.

Raegan: Um….

River: I'm a certified lifeguard. Does that help?

Raegan: Maybe…

River: You'll be perfectly safe. I would never push you to do something you didn't want.

Raegan: Okay. When's your next day off?

River: Sometime next century, I think.

Raegan: ????

River: Never mind. I'll let you know. Sleep tight. Don't let the bedbugs bite.

Raegan: Night, River.

"Well, shit." Pierson looked up again. "I take it there's more?"

"Just one." I didn't see the last one until this morning.

This time I didn't take the phone, just tapped over to the last message.

Ash: I know it's like 3 a.m., but I'm restless. Going for a walk. Wanna join me? I really liked having your company last time. ;)

"Fuckin' hell. You realize you got asked out by three different guys yesterday, right?" Pierson's head jerked up. "Wait. Aren't there four of them living together? The other guy didn't text you too, did he?"

I shook my head. "Z doesn't seem to like me much. As a matter of fact, I'm pretty sure he hates me."

"Okay," Pierson drew the word out as his eyebrows raised. "Well, three guys then, and I think I understand what's going on."

"Really? Are you sure?" I raised my eyebrows at him. "Because I don't think they made it obvious."

"I will push your sarcastic little tush into this fountain," he threatened. "So, the guys might possibly like you."

I pulled a leg up onto the edge of the fountain,

wrapped one arm around it, and trailed my fingers in the water. I knew what he'd ask next.

He didn't disappoint. "The real question is, do you like any of them?"

"Um… Maybe…Yes…"

"Well, see. That's great!" Pierson's face lit up. "Which one?"

I hesitated. Here was my main issue, the reason I was distracted. Maybe talking would help? It couldn't hurt.

"Um...maybe...kind of...um…" I bit my lip and finally squeaked out, "All of them?"

Total silence.

Pierson rubbed his ear and turned his head to the side so he could hear me better. "One more time?"

"All of them?" I squeaked again.

"All. Of. Them," he repeated the words slowly. "Please tell me you're kidding."

I shook my head.

"Well, hell. That complicates things." He held my phone out. "All of them? Really?"

I pulled my hand out of the fountain, shaking it gently to get the water off, to take my phone. "I think so?"

Pierson glared at me.

"I don't know!" Throwing up my hands, I

groaned. "I really, really like Ash, a lot." Heat rose in my cheeks. "But Tarin is sweet and fun, and River is just amazing, and he was so awesome with his little sister. I just… I feel this… I don't know, pull maybe? To all of them. But I don't feel one stronger than the other. I wanna be the one who calms Ash's restlessness. When Tarin has fun, I wanna be there. I wanna play with River's little sister, listen to him sing, and let him teach me to surf. And I wanna get Zephyr to like me…"

My voice trailed off as I fought back tears. I couldn't figure out how I'd ended up here, having feelings for four guys. What the hell was I going to do?

"Wait, even Mr. Grumpy Pants? You like him, too?" When I nodded, he sighed and shook his head. "You really have feelings for all of them, don't you? What are you going to do?"

"I don't know." A tear rolled down my cheek.

Pierson dropped his legs back to the ground to pull me into a hug.

"Common sense says spending more time with each of them would make one stand out, but all I can see are problems with that." I pressed my face against his shoulder. "I mean, wouldn't that be a little like leading them on? And they live together. If I *did* start dating one of them, if I chose one above the others, then it would make things awkward and uncomfortable for everyone else, and it might really hurt them. And I can't stand the thought of that."

The tears were rolling now. "And what would it do to their friendship? I mean, they're so close, and I'd hate to be what tore them apart." I pulled away from him. "And you have no idea how much this has been tearing me up today. It didn't really hit me until this morning how much I felt for them all." In frustration, I punched the stone ledge we sat on, and pain flared through me. "Ah! Fuck!"

"Idiot." Pierson grabbed my hand to checked it over.

I'd gotten off with only a small cut on my knuckles.

He rubbed them, trying to help draw the sting out. "So, what are you thinking?"

Tears still flowed down my cheek. "I'm thinking that I only have one choice. As much as I don't want to, I think…" My breath hitched, and a sob escaped. "I think that I have to stop seeing them, all of them. I've been thinking about it all day, and I can't see any other option. I've been trying to talk myself into telling them. I finally convinced myself that texting, canceling the dates, then ignoring the calls and texts would be easiest, but I can't even manage that. Please, Pierson, please tell me there's another option."

Pierson grabbed my other hand and squeezed. "I wish I could. I really wish I could."

We were so engrossed in conversation that we weren't paying attention to our surroundings until a hand shot out and yanked me off the fountain's edge.

Screeching, I kicked my feet and twisted around, catching a glimpse of all black clothing before I stumbled and fell.

"Rae!" Pierson hollered as the bruising grip yanked me to my feet.

While on the smaller side, the guy who had me was strong, and I stumbled as he tugged me along, pulling me farther into the crowd around the fountain. I tried to yank away, but it was no use, so instead, I thrust out my other hand out, reaching for Pier.

Just out of range, Pierson lunged forward, but someone walked right in front of him, blocking his forward momentum. He snarled, anger and frustration in every line of his tensed body.

Suddenly, the water from the fountain rose in a straight column. The blues swirled together, the column twisting around itself. It curved, and the end pointed. Without warning, it shot out like a whip and slapped at the small, blond man yanking me.

Holy fuck! What was going on? How the hell did that happen?

The wind around me picked up, the breeze seeming to contain me and my captor. The water lashing from the fountain whipped out again, faltering only slightly when it crossed the wind. It wrapped around the arm of my captor and yanked to the side. The arm jerked, but the man held on tight.

When the water lash retreated, I wanted to cry. Then a wave rose and swooped out, drenching us both and shocking the man into letting me go.

I ran to Pierson, who had finally woven through the crowd.

Devin reached us at about the same time. "What the fuck was all that?"

Pierson looked at him, eyes wide as he wrapped me in his arms and hugged me tight. "I have no idea."

I trembled in Pierson's arms, both from adrenaline and the realization I'd been right before.

"There really is no choice," I spoke quietly, more to myself than the boys.

Devin shot me a confused look, but Pierson sighed. "I can't take the chance of one of them getting hurt. I have to stop seeing them."

CHAPTER ELEVEN

ZEPHYR

The still night hung heavy around me. With no moon and a smattering of clouds obscuring the stars, the only real light was the small circles provided by the streetlamps. The shadows seemed deeper, the darkness more ominous.

Of course, it might be the ever-present warning of danger the wind carried since that night at the bowling alley.

Usually, I spent my watches trying to balance burying my paranoia and curing my boredom. Tonight was different. I couldn't put my finger on how. It was more than the warning, more than instinct, more than paranoia. For hours, I'd been on high alert. I felt ridiculous, pacing on the other side of the street and staring up at Raegan's house like some demented stalker, but I also couldn't stop. My whole body felt tight, like a rubber band pulled to its absolute limit.

The others were all sitting at home moping about some texts they all got from Raegan. It sounded like she was putting distance between them, which was none of my business and absolutely didn't add to my irritation. Thinking about the texts that sent my brothers into a panic didn't help.

Why would I care if she broke plans with my friends? Good riddance to the little troublemaker.

Running a hand through my hair, I gave it a sharp tug, hoping to escape my thoughts. My mind was often a dangerous place to be. Usually, when I got like this, River pulled me out, but he wasn't here, so I needed to rely on the only other thing I knew worked. Pain.

After a few hours, I couldn't take it anymore. If I stood here on the other side of the street, I'd end up driving myself to places I didn't need to be going. A quick perimeter check would help, then back to my position. Anything to calm my mind.

When I rounded the side of the house, a shadow flicked across the backyard, one distinctly human-shaped.

It took half a second to decide not to use my

power to stop the shadow. We still hadn't revealed everything to Raegan. I didn't want to take any chances. The last two days had been hard enough.

I ran as quietly as I could until I was inches from the shadow. I reached out and snagged a handful of T-shirt, pulling the shadow to an abrupt halt.

"What the fucking shit?" Pierson yelled as he twisted in my grasp.

Oh, for fuck's sake. This guy again? What the hell was up with him?

"What the fuck are you doing?" I growled as Pierson twisted and smacked me.

When I just stared at him without letting go, he stopped and crossed his arms, glaring right back. "Getting something from my place, you asshole. Let me go!"

"At three in the morning?" I scoffed.

Yeah, not buying it. Why the hell would he be sneaking around instead of just getting it in the morning? While I didn't trust the situation with Raegan, I trusted this guy even less. Something about him bothered me.

The silence stretched a beat too long, so I shook the suspicious little asshole.

"I don't have to explain myself! What the hell are you doing, sneaking around Raegan's house in the middle of the night, huh?" Pierson continued to try and twist out of my hold. "Creepy stalker much?"

With a growl, I shook him again. I wouldn't hurt the kid, but the fucker pissed me off.

Pierson sneered. "You seem extra grumpy tonight. We were watching a movie, for fuck's sake, and I realized I forgot something. Fucking hell! You never stayed up all night watching stupid movies? You need to cool the fuck off!"

A harsh spray of water shot up between us, smacking me in the face.

The shock loosened my grip enough for Pierson to slip free.

I stepped back, out of the spray, gathered the wind, and tried to use it to push against the water. The spray stopped as abruptly as it started, though.

I glared at where Pierson disappeared as I ran a hand over my face to clear off some of the water. Yeah, something was definitely off about him, and it was about damn time to figure it out.

As I took a step to follow and confront him, a breeze brushed past, screaming in my ear.

In the next second, I turned and ran for Raegan's house. I planned to shove air into the lock on the backdoor, but it hung open.

Looked like that idiot, Pierson, might have been telling the truth.

A scream tore through the house and sent a shiver down my spine. I barreled up the stairs. I knew that voice, though I'd never heard it scream.

Doors opened, but I barely registered them. As another scream tore through the house, I gathered the wind around me.

"*Let me go!*" The catch in her voice nearly killed me.

Before I could dwell on that, I caught sight of a guy dressed head to toe in black striding into the hallway, dragging Raegan behind him.

Thrusting my hands out, I directed the wind as I continued to sprint down the hall. I focused the air into a tight tunnel, aiming for the guy's center mass. It was enough to shove him backward, but his grip on Rae stayed strong.

Pounding filled in my ears, and all I could see was the guy holding Rae captive. Turning the wind into small, tight bullets, I pelted the guy to keep him off balance.

The short hall meant it didn't take long for me to get within arm's reach. I let the rage boil over and buried a fist in the guy's face, the wind putting power behind it. I dug the fingers of my other hand into the arm holding Rae, wrapped wind around it, and pressed down hard.

The guy released Rae, and I watched to be sure she got away.

The guy swung at me, face enraged.

Catching the swing, I twisted his arm, wrapped winds around his legs, and pulled, sending him to the ground. Straddling the man, I threw another punch into the guy's face. Fury clouded my senses, but I didn't care. If this guy thought he could take Rae, I would disabuse him of that notion.

I drove a fist into the guy's stomach, then another, and another. I sent the wind in small, rapid bullets into the guy's face. The wind swirled and howled, tightening around us, following the focus of my ire. The wind circled tighter around the guy as my fists continued to fly into him.

"Zephyr!"

I heard the shout, but I didn't stop.

"Zephyr!"

I ignored it again. This guy wouldn't escape after what he did. He wouldn't get another chance at Rae.

"Z." The soft touch on the back of my shoulder stilled my fists as much as the whisper in my ear.

Glancing over my shoulder, I found Raegan

staring at the guy who'd tried to take her, expression dismayed.

"Z," she said gently. "I don't think he can breathe."

What was she talking about?

When I glanced back at the guy, a jolt went through me at the sight of his blue lips. I drew back the wind in a rush that made my head hurt. Since the guy wasn't going anywhere, I stood and gathered Rae against me. Burying my face in her hair, I stayed there until my anger drained away.

"It's okay, Z. I'm okay," Rae murmured against my chest. Her hand stroked in time to her words as she repeated them over and over.

"What the flaming fuck bunnies?" Devin's voice cut through my haze.

Jerking back, I released my hold on Rae and fixed an impassive look on my face as I took in Rae's brother and parents staring at me.

"I'd kind of like the answer to that, too." Rae's voice was quieter but no less confused.

Well, shit.

My eyes slid over to Rae's parents, asking silent permission.

Her dad nodded.

I pulled my phone out and shot off a quick text to

the others. It would appear the time had finally come to reveal ourselves, whether or not we thought she was ready.

"Devin, take your sister downstairs. We'll be having company soon." Raegan's dad never took his eyes off the man groaning on the floor.

Devin did as asked, gently grabbing Rae's arm and leading her down the stairs. The moment Rae's head disappeared from view, her mother gave a strangled sob and crumpled against her husband.

"Should we call the police?" Rae's dad asked.

I shook my head. "Not necessary. Tarin already has."

It was a half-truth. Tarin called the Lex, who would pretend to be police. We were all convinced that whoever was behind the kidnap attempts wasn't an ordinary human.

Picking up the mumbling sack of shit, I flung him over a shoulder, none too gently. Just for fun, I made a point of hitting every step hard on the way down the stairs, then dumped him unceremoniously on the floor without even looking when I made it to the kitchen.

I found the damn scruffy blond currently hugging Raegan. Hadn't I watched this guy take off? What the fuck was he doing back here?

"Raegan texted him," Devin said quietly. "He's her rock. She's always going to turn to him when she's in trouble."

I scowled. She had Tarin, Ash, and River now. She didn't need some weirdo with purple chunks in his hair.

A knock on the door made Rae jump in Pierson's arms.

A minute later, Rae's dad led Tarin, Ash, River, and two Lex into the kitchen. None of the guys said a word as they spread out around the kitchen. The Lex officers cuffed Rae's attacker and asked a few short questions before saying they'd be back tomorrow.

When they'd left, Rae's parents sank into chairs at the table, clearly exhausted. Devin started coffee, brought them both a cup, then settled into a chair as well.

"Now, will someone tell us what the hell all that was upstairs?" Devin asked, his voice soft but determined. He wanted answers.

Rae's parents looked over at us. They wanted answers too, though I suspected their questions might be a bit different.

With a sigh, I ran a hand through my hair, tugging it at the end, then pushed off the counter I'd been leaning on. "I assume you're asking about my actions."

Devin shook his head. "Not exactly. I know a few things about fighting. You were hitting that guy good, but he wasn't breathing. Nothing you'd done, no punch you'd thrown, would have done that to him. So, what I want to know first is why the hell did he quit breathing? My second question is why the hell was there a goddamn windstorm in the middle of the fucking hallway? And my third, most important question, is why the fuck were you so conveniently nearby?"

Devin's voice rose with every question until he was shouting. His hands slammed down on the table, and his glare focused in my direction.

"The wind was me," I said simply.

Devin stilled, then shot his parents a glance. I couldn't read what passed between them, but Devin sunk back into his chair.

I was not good with families. Someone else should take over. I shot a desperate glance at the others.

River stepped forward, so I went back to leaning against the counter. I'd had more than enough family interaction for one night. Hell, one lifetime. Plus, this way I could keep an eye on

Pierson. The little shit was too friendly with Raegan.

"We"—River indicated himself as well as me, Tarin, and Ash— "are not exactly human." His words got Devin's, Rae's, and Pierson's attention. "We are Elementum."

"Elementals?" Pierson muttered, making it sound like a question.

"Sure, if that's easier. It's not what we call ourselves, but it's a good word to help you understand what we are. Elementum are born with the ability to control one of the four elements of nature." River pointed to each of us in turn. "Earth, Fire, Wind," he pointed to himself. "Water. Those are the elements we control. We have different names, but our terms for things are unimportant to this discussion. Each of us can control and manipulate an element, and together, we form a complete quad of elements, a Genus."

The three of them didn't believe him.

River looked at Ash, who nodded. This would be good. I knew what would happen next. They'd done it to entertain Bethie plenty of times.

Grabbing a glass and filling it with water, I set it down in front of River as Ash pulled his ever-present lighter from his pocket.

"I guess seeing is believing," River said.

He held his hand over the glass, several inches of air between them by necessity. As he rolled his hand around, the water in the glass rose until it was nearly level with River's hand. On the next twist of his hand, River caught the water, formed it into a ball, then caught up a little more and a little more until he had something roughly the size of a baseball.

Across from him, Ash twisted his hand over the flame of his lighter several times, until a ring of fire formed.

River tossed his water ball a few times, catching it in the same hand, then suddenly twisted and lobbed the water ball at Ash.

Ash sent his fire ring at River. The water ball passed through the fire ring seamlessly before both of them canceled their powers. The fire vanished and the water splashed onto the counter.

They turned back to the now silent table.

A moment later, Raegan stood and started walking off.

Ash ran over and caught her wrist gently, stopping her. "Where are you going?"

Rae looked at him, eyebrows raised. "I'm going to find a closet." Confusion brought Ash's brows together. "Why?"

"Because I want to leave Narnia, thank you very much," she replied, as though it should be obvious.

Ash lost it and pulled Raegan into a hug even as he shook with laughter. "Oh my elements, I think I love you."

I was pretty sure she muttered, "Bastard," under her breath.

Ash led her back to the table, sitting down himself and pulling her into his lap.

Stupid fuck, getting all goofy over this troublemaker.

"So, what the fuck does you guys being all Harry Potterish have to do with *my sister*?" Devin demanded, breaking out of his stunned silence.

For fuck's sake, the guy needed to stop shouting.

Ash spoke up. "Because she's an Elementum."

"What?" Pierson squeaked.

"It's true," Rae's mom said.

I had wondered how long it would take one of her parents to kick into this conversation.

"So, then, what's her element?" Pierson asked.

Devin appeared to be in shock.

"We don't know," Tarin said. "We are trying to find out. All we know is that she bonded with us four, so she belongs to us."

"*What the fuck*?" Rae shot to standing, leaving

137

Ash with raised eyebrows. Her face twisted with a scowl, and irritation flared in her eyes. "I don't belong to anyone, Tarin!" She stormed over to him, poking her finger against his chest. "I am my own person and don't you forget it, you insensitive pig. And the rest of you!" She whirled around, spearing each of us with her glare. "Sitting around and talking about me like I'm not here."

Heh, I kinda liked a pissed-off troublemaker. Maybe I needed to piss her off more.

She whirled again, this time spearing her parents with her glare. "And keeping secrets from me? Secrets about me. Don't you think I had a right to know what you apparently know? And that's even if I believe for one goddamn second that I am what you say I am. It's not enough to have someone try three different times to kidnap me. No, now I have to supposedly be some kind of freak?"

She spun back to Tarin to glare up at him. "And I suppose next you'll be telling me all about how I was the only member of my family to survive some horrid attack? Isn't that how it always goes in these stories? I mean, if we're gonna play this—"

Tarin cut off her tirade by bending to press his lips against hers.

She punched his chest once, twice, then melted

into him. Her hands flattened against his chest as she leaned into him, kissing him back.

My gut twisted uncomfortably as I watched them.

When they broke apart, her face was flushed, her lips swollen, eyes bright. She blinked a few times before coming back to herself.

Blushing, she pushed away from Tarin and returned to the table.

Was I the only one bothered by what had just happened? Was it really that I minded? I didn't care about the girl, so what the hell was going on with me?

River seemed unfazed, which didn't mean anything. He had a good poker face. Ash, though, was sending murderous glares in Tarin's direction.

Well, that was no surprise. What the hell had Tarin been thinking, kissing her in front of Ash? We all knew Ash had a massive crush on her. He hadn't said as much, but he hadn't needed to. It had been fairly obvious.

River gave Tarin another glance, then shook his head as he turned back to the table. He could deal with those two. I didn't want to get between them.

"Raegan, I know this is unsettling, and a huge adjustment, but I'm afraid that there's more," River said. "We're pretty sure the person behind the kidnappings is a Furcifer, an Elementum criminal, if you will. Your parents asked us to keep watch on the house at night after the first attack, but it's time to change things a bit. You'll be better off moving in with us."

"Moving in?" Rae's voice held a note of hesitation.

I figured it had something to do with whatever had made her send those texts two days ago, which I still didn't care about.

"Mom? Dad?" She turned to find them both nodding.

"I think he's right, honey." Her mom reached over and patted Rae's hand as she smiled.

Rae's face turned to stone. She stood slowly, putting both palms on the table. "Well, since you all have my life planned out for me, I'll be in my room. Let me know which one of you I'm supposed to marry, won't you? It'll save me some trouble." She whirled and stormed off up the stairs.

Ash popped out of his chair and made to dash after her, but Pierson caught his arm.

"Not a good idea, man." He shook his head. "When she's in this kind of mood, it's better to let her stew for a while."

The desire to growl rose inside, and I wanted to say something nasty and hateful. Instead, I clenched my fists tight at my sides. Rae had retreated, and with her, the reason for this little meeting.

I pushed away from the counter. "I'm going the fuck home."

Before I do something I'll regret, and Rae won't forgive.

River tossed the keys to the SUV at me. I hurried out, making a point to not look at Pierson.

If I did, I didn't think I'd be able to contain myself.

CHAPTER TWELVE

RAEGAN

"It's not the end of the world, honey." Mom's chuckle didn't make her words reassuring.

I still wasn't pleased they kept secrets from me, secrets *about* me, for crying out loud! At least, we finally talked about it, and I understand why they'd kept it from me. They wanted me to have a normal life, and they didn't know much to start with. But it didn't stop the hurt.

I'd spent the rest of the week packing, and when Saturday afternoon rolled around, I was ready to go.

"Really, Mom?" I shot her a stony glare for that comment. "Do you have any idea how many of those apocalyptic books I've read start with that line? It's a phrase practically guaranteed to ensure horrible events will ensue, and you have to go and utter it on the day I move out." I threw my hands in the air in mock exasperation. "Are you trying to get me killed?"

"Eight point five. Not bad, baby, but the arm thing at the end was a little much," Ash quipped with a grin as he strolled by with a box meant for Tarin's waiting truck.

Fucking hell. Of course, he caught me being a drama queen.

"My sister, Farrah, would have done better. More over the top," Tarin called as he swung down from the truck.

These boys were trying to kill me. Tarin had removed his shirt, and my brain refused to work as I took in the expanse of well-muscled, gleaming, mocha skin suddenly on display. He shifted to take the box Ash handed to him, muscles flexing.

I wiped the corner of my mouth to be sure I wasn't drooling. How the hell was I gonna live with that on display twenty-four seven?

River came out next with another box and snorted. "Bethie might only be three, but I'm pretty sure she can beat them both in the drama queen race."

Despite being unhappy about this whole forced move thing, I loved being included in their easy camaraderie. The boys were trying to make this easier on me, for which I was grateful.

"Can we cut the bullshit and just get this done?" Zephyr snapped as he carried out another box. "I have a job later."

Okay, so most of them tried to make things easier. I couldn't figure out what bug had crawled up Zephyr's ass. One moment he was beating a man near to death for attacking me, and the next he was back to acting like he couldn't stand to be near me.

Maybe he was afraid of me? I laughed silently at the thought. I had enough to deal with, a whole new world to acclimate to. There was already too much going on to be worried about figuring out my grumpy, new roommate.

With the four guys plus Devin, my stuff was loaded in short order, and we were ready to head out. Pierson was at a soccer game and wasn't able to help see me off, leaving me feeling slightly abandoned as I was basically being kicked out of my home.

Devin dragged me into a tight hug. "I still don't like this, but maybe they're right. Please be careful and don't be stupid." He glanced over to where the guys waited. "And try not to get your heart broken. I'd hate to have to end any of them."

I laughed. My brother was ridiculous.

Devin ran a hand over the unfinished dreamcatcher on my shoulder blade. "We still have to finish this. It's not colored in or anything, so call the parlor and make an appointment with me, okay?"

I nodded, my throat tight. The day I'd gotten the dreamcatcher was etched into my memory. Devin had talked me into getting the tattoo. I'd only agreed if he would be the one doing it, since I knew his work. I'd intended to do a small butterfly until I looked through Devin's artbook and the dreamcatcher caught my eye.

It was beautiful, with each of the four elements represented at the axis and would be stunning once he finished it. We made a point, though, of only working on it at the tattoo parlor he worked at, which required me to make an appointment.

People sometimes thought he was scary with the piercings, tattoos, and goth clothes, but my brother was a giant softie. I'd miss him so much.

Finally releasing me, Devin shoved me at our parents.

I gave them each a quick hug before I climbed into the truck with Tarin. River, and Ash, and Zephyr followed in the SUV.

A hand closed over mine, and I glanced down to find Tarin had laced our fingers together.

A tiny thrill ran up my spine. When I looked back at the Bronco, I noticed Ash glaring in our direction.

This was why I'd sent the text, why I'd pulled away from them, to prevent any tension between them.

Things didn't get any better when we started unloading things at the house, either.

Tarin helped me out of the truck, a quick peck on my lips taking me by surprise. I didn't even have time to respond. It didn't stop Ash's glare, or River's sigh, or… Well, Z was always prickly, so no change there.

My cheeks heated as I grabbed a box out of the back. Even though we worked in silence, the guys moved as if they could read each other's minds. I ended up more in the way than helping, so eventually, I gave up and let them go at it.

As I watched them, my thoughts drifted to Tarin.

We hadn't spoken about the kiss in the kitchen the night I discovered I was an Elementum. I'd been too mad, then too busy packing to talk to any of the guys. Did he assume my response to his skillful lips meant I was okay will more kisses? Was I now his girlfriend? No, that's something we definitely would have talked about, right? Maybe kissing is a casual thing for him? Sure, that sounded reasonable. It likely meant nothing to him. Which is how I needed it to be. I already made the decision not to pursue anything romantic with any of them, and I have the texts to remind myself if I falter.

When a few boxes were in my new room, I decided to unpack.

The guys obviously prepped my room for me, and I was thankful for that since I didn't have to haul my furniture over from my parent's house. They'd brought in a lovely, dark wood bed with a matching dresser and nightstand. The simple lines of the furniture made them unisex, and I wondered if they'd pulled it from somewhere else. Over the dresser, they hung a large oval mirror, and in one corner was a simple desk.

Despite the tension still hanging in the air, the guys' ability to work together perfectly meant the truck emptied in no time.

Tarin brought in a box, set it down, came over, then wrapped his arms around me, hugging me tight against him.

A shiver raced down my spine, and I leaned into him. I shouldn't have—it was counterproductive to my goals—but I couldn't help it. I loved the feel of being wrapped in Tarin's strong arms.

"We should talk," Tarin whispered, warm breath

ghosting across my ear and doing nothing for the shivers he caused.

I knew what he wanted to talk about, and it couldn't happen. Not the talk, not what he wanted. Nothing good would come of it. I would ruin everything, cause damage to this wonderful friendship, to the special nature of the guys' relationship, one I barely understood. I needed to avoid this talk.

Pulling out of Tarin's arms, I turned, and my eyes nearly popped out of my head when I noticed Ash's hard glare. My expression and my squeak caused Tarin to look over his shoulder.

"Hey, Ash," he said it almost dismissively, then turned back and ran a finger over my cheek. "We'll talk after dinner, Sunshine."

He left me with Ash, whose expression changed from a glare to completely blank.

I wanted to hug him, kiss him, hold him. I wanted to reassure him everything would be fine. What was wrong with me that I could go from enjoying Tarin's affection to wanting to kiss Ash in the blink of an eye?

Ash set down the box he held. "That's the last of it. I'm going to take a shower."

I didn't miss the hurt and irritation in his voice.

CHAPTER THIRTEEN

ASH

I t took a lot of effort to refrain from slamming the door to the bathroom.

I knew the green-eyed monster eating me didn't have a right to be there. After all, I hadn't told the others my intentions, but I didn't think I needed to. I figured they'd see how much I liked Rae. In the two years we'd been a complete Genus, we'd functioned on an intuitive level, better than some Genus who'd been together for decades.

My sister's was the only other Genus I knew who functioned on our level.

Stripping, I stepped into the shower and tossed my clothes in the nearby hamper. As the shower head beat down on me in tiny rivers, I let thoughts of Rae invade. I couldn't have mistaken what I felt.

From the moment I'd met her eyes as I helped her off the ground, there'd been a connection between us. It grew stronger the more time we spent together.

I'd never dated anyone seriously before. I slept with girls here and there to scratch an itch, but things were different when it came to Rae. None of those other girls held a candle to her, and I'd been working up the nerve to ask her out.

Tarin had to know how much I liked her. We'd been best friends since we were in diapers. Tarin making moves on Rae was like a stab to the gut, and I didn't know what to do with that feeling. It didn't make a lick of sense.

Polyamory wasn't exactly rare among Elementum. I mean, fuck, my sister had three boyfriends, and two of them were dating each other as well. The four of them were committed to their relationship. If Tarin actually was interested, I needed to let these jealous and betrayed feelings go.

Really, I needed to let it go regardless. It wasn't up to me who Rae dated. That was solely up to her.

A short time later, I stepped out of the shower, feeling a thousand times better. After sweating all afternoon. I'd been schlepping boxes at Forever Home before meeting up with the others to help Rae move in. I'd smelled like a horse's behind. Horse's behind, to be specific.

The shower cooled my head enough to let me decide I'd keep pursuing Rae. What I felt for her was more than our bond snapping into place, and if I'd learned anything from my sister last year, it was not to fight what you felt. I would keep being me and let the pieces fall where they may.

Giving myself a quick dry, I hung the towel on the silver bar next to the shower after, knowing Zephyr would have a fit if I left it on the floor. The only one who didn't hang their towel was River. He left a disaster in the bathroom designed to send Zephyr into a mumbling, cleaning frenzy. I couldn't figure out if he did it on purpose or not.

I glanced in the mirror, then ran my fingers through my hair to spike it up a bit. The movement brought my unfinished tattoo sleeve to my attention. I wanted to finish it, get it colored, but I was picky and hadn't found anyone I trusted since my last tattoo artist moved.

Flipping on the exhaust fan—something else Zephyr insisted we do—I strode out of the bathroom.

Halfway to my room, Raegan came out of her own.

I flashed her a grin. "Hey, Rae."

She froze, her eyes flitting quickly down. Her pretty, pale gray eyes widened as they fixed on a low point on my body.

With what sounded like a strangled squeak, she turned and ran into her room.

What the hell was up with her? A glance down revealed I'd left the bathroom stark naked. Well shit. That explained why she freaked.

I strode into my room, snatched up a pair of boxer briefs, and slid them on. I imagined the sight was shocking if you'd never seen one. This was a good chance to hang out a bit, just the two of us.

When I reached Rae's room, I found her standing in the middle, still processing or something. I'd steal this chance to flirt and fluster her.

"So, Rae," I said as I walked to her bed and collapsed onto her pink, white, and gold comforter with a huge grin and a wink. "I take it that's the first one you've ever seen?"

The blush spreading over her cheeks was adorable.

She blinked several times, before coming to sit on the bed with me, tucking her legs under herself like a cat curling up for a nap.

"Y...Yes," she stammered out, swallowing and picking at imaginary lint on her comforter.

Could the girl get any cuter? Shit, she was killing me already, and she'd just moved in.

"It's called an apadravya piercing," I said, referring to the silver bar threaded from top to bottom through the head of Little Ash.

Raegan relaxed as I told her about the piercing and ignored her seeing me in my birthday suit. Part of me wanted to tease her and ask if she'd liked what she saw, but that wouldn't go over well.

Her fingers stilled, though the color was still in her cheeks, as she finally lifted her gaze to mine. "Did it hurt?"

Her face scrunched up when she asked it, and I laughed, unable to help myself. It was that or kiss her.

"Baby, I had a needle stuck through my dick." Sitting up, my shoulders shook as I put a finger under her chin to keep her from looking away in embarrassment. "It hurt like fuckin' hell. I thought I was going to die."

The red on her cheeks deepened. "That was kind of a stupid question, wasn't it?"

Fuck, this girl already had me wrapped around her finger.

"I'm teasing, baby," I admitted. "It hurt, sure, but no worse than anything else I'd done to my body at that point." The sharp sting when she smacked me came as a shock. "Ouch!"

"What the hell are you doing in her room in your goddamn underwear, Ash?" The growl came from the doorway.

We twisted around to find Zephyr glaring at us from the doorway.

I wished he'd tone down his assholish tendencies around Rae. Zephyr didn't trust easily. The only one who had gotten past all the walls he built was River. That wasn't to say Zephyr didn't trust me or Tarin, he did, but River seemed to connect to him on a level that we couldn't.

I grinned and lounged back against the pillows with my hands behind my head. "Just getting to know our new roomie. Nothing wrong with that, is there?"

Zephyr rolled his eyes. "Go put pants on, moron."

"Killjoy," I muttered as I got up and headed back to my room.

CHAPTER FOURTEEN

RAEGAN

I tried to hide my nervous giggles as Zephyr turned back to me and shook his head. "Look, Rae. Ash is a good guy and all, just don't get too attached, okay?"

What the hell did he mean by that?

"Why not?" I asked. "And who said I was?"

"No one said, but you looked kind of cozy. And why not? Because Ash goes through women faster than most women go through shoes. He'll break your heart." Zephyr turned and left after dropping that little bomb.

What did he intend by telling me that? Was he really looking out for me, or was something else behind his advice? He'd been the hardest to get to know, and even now, I didn't know how to act around him. He was surly and distrustful, but he relaxed with River around.

Needing someone to talk to, I pulled my phone out and dialed the one person who wasn't connected to the crazy my life had become.

I breathed a sigh of relief as the musical tenor voice washed over me.

"Hey, beautiful, what's new?" Pierson greeted.

I flopped back on my bed. "I'm, um, all moved."

"That was fast," he said in surprise. "Guess all that muscle helped, huh? So, when can I come see your new digs?"

Zephyr made no secret that he didn't like Pierson. Maybe I should ease him into my best friend coming over.

"I don't... I don't think that's a great idea, Pier. Not right now, okay?" I spoke softly, uncertain of how he'd take it.

He knew everything I did. He'd arrived in the aftermath of that night and heard everything, but I didn't know how much I wanted to drag him into whatever world I'd been pulled into.

"Rae-Rae, we swore nothing would change when you moved." He didn't sound upset, just stating a fact.

Thank God he understood.

"I know, and I meant it, but just… Let me get settled with the guys first." I lowered my voice. "I'm still not sure if Zephyr likes me."

Pierson laughed. "From what I've seen, I don't think Zephyr likes anyone. Maybe he's just pissed that he got stuck with a name like Zephyr. Who does that to a kid?"

Personally, I thought the name suited him, but I wouldn't admit that.

With my door open, I heard movement in the kitchen and glanced at the clock, startled to find it was already five at night.

"I should go see if I can help with dinner." Even though I muttered, Pierson and his supersonic ears heard me.

"You go make nice with the new roomies. Call me tomorrow," he instructed. "Love ya."

"Yeah, okay, love ya, too." Hanging up, I tossed the phone on the nightstand before heading for the kitchen.

Ash leaned against the wall opposite my door, dressed this time, with his face scrunched up.

My stomach churned at his obvious annoyance.

"Are you going to help with dinner, or are you going to meet your little boyfriend?" Ash growled in a remarkable imitation of Zephyr before he turned and stormed back to his room.

I stared after him, wishing I knew how to navigate this minefield of guys.

After a couple of minutes, I gave up trying to understand them and headed downstairs to help with dinner. I never wanted to be the quiet, background girl, and in the past, I made a point of ensuring I was always heard and seen.

Except now, I was in a new and very strange world where I didn't know the rules or even how any of this was supposed to work. While I didn't want to come across as shy or awkward, I didn't want to do anything offensive, either, so I tried to stay out of the way as much as possible and pitch in where it was obviously something I could do.

When Ash came down to join everyone in the kitchen, he slid in seamlessly, knowing his place among the group.

Watching the boys in the kitchen was a unique experience and gave me some insight into how they worked. The most obvious thing was how they all seemed to micromanage River, especially Zephyr.

Like right now when River moved to the stove and began stirring the sauce, Zephyr came up behind him and pressed a hand to the small of his back before reaching around and grabbing the wooden spoon. After tapping on the rim of the pot, he set it down on a folded paper towel on the counter, then he shifted River to the side, picked up the spoon again, tasted the sauce, muttered something to River, and led him over to the sink.

The thing that stood out to me the most was that Zephyr's hand never left the small of River's back.

River began rinsing the dishes and setting them in the dishwasher. At this point, there wasn't a lot to do. Spaghetti wasn't exactly a labor-intensive dish. I'd chopped onions and garlic for the sauce already; Zephyr was keeping half an eye on the pots while wiping down counters.

Zephyr seemed to like things very tidy and clean.

Tarin was grilling some sausage outside.

When I'd asked about that, Tarin shrugged and said, "Why not?"

Hard to argue with that.

Ash was making more coffee after draining the last of the previous pot himself.

The next time River wandered to the stove, Ash shoved a cup of coffee in his hands and steered him to the table where I was putting a salad together.

I couldn't help the laugh that escaped. "Got kicked out?"

River sank into the chair next to me with a shrug. "Yeah. They don't trust me in the kitchen."

"You burned water!" Ash set a cup of coffee down in front of me, his previous bad mood forgotten. "Creamer? Sugar?"

I nodded, and he headed to the fridge.

"How does one burn water? Can't you control water?"

River sank a bit in his chair. "Don't ask."

Tarin strolled in with the delicious scent of grilled sausage wafting ahead of him. Zephyr transferred the sauce to the pot with the noodles, mixed them up, and brought them to the table while Tarin set the sausages down.

I expected the guys to be loud and annoying at dinner, but they didn't talk much at all. Zephyr rested an elbow on the back of River's chair, and other than that, the boys basically dug in, ate like someone would take the food away in five minutes, then dispersed after rinsing their dishes and putting them in the dishwasher.

While I applauded their ability to clean up after themselves, I was going to have to teach them about having a proper dinnertime.

Since I still felt a bit awkward in the house, I retreated to my room for the evening. I played a game on my phone for a bit, texted with Pier about his soccer game and the shows we were streaming, fiddled with my stuff, and generally kept busy.

It didn't take long for the day to catch up to me. My brain still wanted to worry, but I forced it to shut down as I crawled under my comforter.

Tomorrow was soon enough to figure things out.

The sun shining directly into my eyes woke me the next morning.

Reluctantly, I climbed out of bed and threw on some yoga pants and a tank top. I didn't have any plans today except to get settled in.

Voices led me downstairs to the kitchen. I stood in the entry, watching in amazement as the guys moved effortlessly around each other. It was like they knew every movement the others would make. They'd worked this way last night, too, but uncaffeinated me found their ability to do this first thing in the morning nothing short of a miracle.

Zephyr placed the pot of sugar in front of Ash without being asked while Tarin set eggs in front of River. They were talking the whole time, too.

Okay, maybe it was more like arguing.

"I don't think we're ready for that yet," Tarin said.

"We need to be proactive. Someone tried to take her three times!" Ash shouted. "You think we should just sit around and let them try again? What if they succeed this time, huh? What then?"

"I never said that, Ash," Tarin protested. "We need to think about this, though. We still don't know what her element is."

"We need to act, not think!" Ash glared at him. "Or maybe you were hoping to do other things?"

"Ash." River placed a hand on Ash's shoulder. "I think you need to calm down."

He shrugged off River's touch. "No, what I need is to feel like we're doing something to protect Rae!"

"We *are* doing something. We brought her here." Tarin seemed calm, but irritation was slipping into his voice.

He was getting irked, fast.

"And what? We're just supposed to parade around like a bunch of Neanderthals protecting the dainty princess in the tower?" Ash threw up his hands. "Don't you think Rae deserves for us to treat her with more respect than that? To treat her like an equal? Not some mindless boob who can't figure out how to protect herself?"

"You're putting words in my mouth!" Tarin's voice

rose, not quite shouting, but close. "I know how capable she is!"

I clutched the wall next to me, my knees trembling. This was exactly what I'd been hoping to avoid. The argument sounded okay at first, but now, every word shot out of their mouths like bullets. I didn't want this. How did I fix this?

A pair of sea-green eyes suddenly met mine.

"Dweebs!" Zephyr shouted to get their attention.

Tarin and Ash both shot him a glare.

Zephyr pointed a finger in my direction. "There's a lady present."

Both of them went still and silent.

Ash turned, face pale and eyes wide.

I was in full tremble now. I bit my bottom lip and could feel the sting of tears building in my eyes. I could not cry in front of these guys!

"Baby, I'm sorry," Ash whispered just loud enough for me to hear.

I swallowed, unable to do more than hold back the tears that continued to threaten.

Ash flicked his tongue out, running the bar in it over his bottom lip as he glanced at the others in desperation.

Tarin remained frozen, gaze fixed on me.

Zephyr, of course, scowled and returned to his chai tea.

Finally, River stood, rolling his eyes at the others. He crossed the small kitchen and put one hand on my shoulder, the other cupping my cheek.

"Hey," his voice was soft and even as he tilted my head to look at him. "It's not a big thing, okay? Just guys being guys. If they were really fighting, I would have stepped in. This is just, you know, normal family stuff. We're just trying to figure out what the best course of action is. But the person whose voice needs to be heard most is yours. It's your life we've taken over without asking, and that should stop here." He brushed his thumb over my cheek, wiping away the stray tear that had leaked out. "So, why don't we take a couple deep breaths, calm down, and head to the table?"

I followed his lead into some deep breathing.

In moments, I felt the tears retreat and calm return.

River took my hand and led me to the table, sitting me next to him. A mug was plopped down in front of me, and I glanced up to see Zephyr.

"Thank you." My voice was soft and still a bit rough from sleep.

"Whatever," Zephyr grunted as he sat back down

with his own mug freshly steaming. "Playtime's over, you two. Sit the fuck down."

Tarin and Ash both sat.

For several minutes, silence prevailed, and I was glad for it. At least, no one was shouting anymore. I still had difficulty believing everything they said was real. It had been the middle of the night, after all. Surely it had just been hallucinations brought on by sleep deprivation, or something.

Right?

"All right, we really do need to figure this out." River finally spoke up since it appeared no one else was going to. "You both had valid points. I'd feel better knowing Raegan could at least use her powers, but we don't know what her element is. How do we train an element we don't know?"

"Um?" I nervously interrupted. "How do we even know I have powers? I've never felt anything different, and you all said you didn't know. I mean, could whoever gave me to my parents have been mistaken? I just... This all seems like a bit much to believe."

I was too tired to put on all the bravado I had the other night, and I really didn't want another fight to start. If that meant playing the meek, awkward girl, then I would.

For now, anyway.

Another silence fell, this one shorter than the first.

"Then, how about a little show?" Ash asked, his grin back in place. "Let us show you what we can do. It might help you feel your own element more. At the very least, it will prove this isn't one big hallucination and give you an idea about how everything works. I mean, our world—*your* world—is more complicated than we could do in one quick show, but it might at least provide an introduction." Ash practically bounced in his chair.

"Okay." I grinned at his exuberance.

"Yes! Come on. Let's head down to the basement." Ash shot out of his chair and tugged at my hand.

"Dishes!" Zephyr growled at him.

With a huff, Ash released me to grab his mug and plate and rinsed them off.

The others did the same, then we trooped down to the basement.

I had certain expectations of basements. They were supposed to be small, dark, cramped, creepy, poorly lit, musty, dank, and overall horrible places to be in.

What I walked into was nothing like that. The walls were exposed brick in varying shades of red, with some burnt nearly black, and the floor was concrete. As I walked, I noticed the floor had a subtle slope to it and a drain in the middle. There were no windows, but globe lights in the corners provided more than enough light.

Mats like what could be found at a gym or martial arts place were stacked in one corner next to a silver, two-door cabinet. A fire extinguisher hung on the wall near the entrance. Another corner was filled with weights, while a small fan and several large potted plants sat on a table nearby. A couple of chairs that looked as if they once belonged to the table upstairs completed the setup.

"What is this place?" I asked.

"Our training room." Ash motioned to the chairs. "Just sit and let us show off."

I sat as the guys gathered near the table and talked for a minute. Seeing them all together like that made my heart stutter and trip. They were all so wonderful, so unique, and so handsome. How was I ever going to handle being around them all the time?

The guys separated, with Tarin grabbing one of the plants and setting it on the floor near me. It was a pretty large, wide pot, ceramic maybe, with gray and green swirls decorating the outside. A tiny green shoot stuck up a couple inches out of the dark potting soil.

Tarin crouched in front of the pot, then looked up at me.

I had to remind myself how to breathe when I saw the intensity of his dark gaze.

"Okay, Sunshine. I'm Terra—"

"I thought you were Tarin?" I interrupted, putting emphasis on the *N*.

Tarin looked stunned.

I couldn't help bursting out in laughter. "I'm kidding. Terra is Latin for Earth, right?"

The other guys chuckled, and Tarin turned red as he nodded.

"So, um, I can manipulate earth." Tarin stumbled over his words a bit before seeming to regain confidence. "That's the key, manipulate not create. I can't just form a ball of dirt out of thin air."

Zephyr snorted a laugh. "I don't know why not. I can form a ball of my element out of thin air." Which, of course, he then did. A tiny, swirling ball of air spun in his palm for a moment before he snuffed out.

"Cheater," Tarin mumbled.

I bit my lip to keep my grin from breaking loose as I watched Tarin.

For a moment, Tarin didn't seem to do anything, simply stared at the plant in front of him. Then, the plant began to grow. The green stalk shot up, leaves unfurling, and finally a beautiful bloom I didn't recognize unfurled.

My mouth fell open in astonishment, but Tarin wasn't done.

He pointed a finger at the pot of soil and began moving it in a circle. As I watched, a trench formed in the soil, in a circle around the flower, growing wider and deeper with every pass of Tarin's finger. He stopped when he'd finally created a mini moat, sans water, around the flower.

He grinned as he sat back on his heels.

I had a million questions with no idea where to start.

It must have shown, because Tarin held up a hand to keep me from talking. "It's limited to my own power level and training level. A flower like this, or moving a small amount of dirt, is rather easy. I couldn't take a tree sapling and make it the size of the ones you find in forests. I honestly don't know of any Terra who has that much power. It's difficult to manipulate on that kind of level. Nature is fickle. It doesn't like to be changed. It can, and does, fight against it. This isn't the only thing I can do. Every Elementum type has abilities that are unique to it, but outside of manipulation of the element. I can't really demonstrate mine, but I can communicate telepathically with animals."

Tarin grinned at me as he stood, grabbed the pot, and put it back on the table. If he could communicate with animals, did that mean he could talk to Horse at the shelter? That would be incredible.

River stepped in front of me as Tarin slouched on the floor, using the wall as a backrest.

"Um, wait. I still have questions," I protested as I leaned forward to see around him.

"We know, but hold on to them, okay? You may have more or get some answers before we're done," River said.

I nodded and leaned back.

"Now, you've seen what I can do. The other night and, um, at the park," he said, darting a glance at the other guys.

My eyes widened as I finally put together what had really happened at the park that day when the water swirled around my ankles like an infinity symbol. I hadn't given it much thought since then, to be honest, too wrapped up in my worry.

"So, my other ability probably won't be a big surprise." He took the glass of water Zephyr handed him.

I hadn't even noticed him filling it.

River put his hand over the glass and made a motion like he was pulling the water out of it. The water rose out of the glass. He gathered it into a ball like he had the other night, but instead of a swirling ball of water, it froze. River wasn't done, though. He handed the now empty glass back to Zephyr, then started playing with the ball of ice. His motions were quick and small, so I really couldn't see what exactly he was doing.

After a few moments, he stopped and turned the ball of ice toward me.

I burst out laughing at the comical little grumpy face now carved into the ice.

He lobbed the ball over his shoulder blindly. An outraged shout from Zephyr as the ball unfroze and soaked him had me clutching my stomach and trying not to fall off the chair.

Zephyr shot River a glare as he went to the cabinet and pulled out a towel.

River dropped into the chair next to me, and Zephyr rolled his eyes and stepped forward. "All this showing off is stupid, but whatever. You saw the little ball of air, so do I really need to show you again?" I shook my head, grinning at Zephyr's grumpiness. For some reason, I found it adorable. "Good, then we'll move the fuck on. My other ability—"

Zephyr stopped abruptly and spun, flinging his hands out in front of him as if he could stop the ball of fire barreling down on him.

I held my breath, afraid he wouldn't move in time. Then, the fireball fizzled out just a foot in front of Zephyr.

"Thanks, Ash-hole," Zephyr said as he spun back around. "Sphere of protection. I can only do it when in imminent danger, and it's limited to about two people, though I can project it to others. So, I can protect two people other than myself."

Without another word, Zephyr took up his previous wall-leaning position.

A part of me wanted to go over there and do something drastic to break through that grumpy facade, but I didn't think slapping him was a bright idea.

Ash stepped forward now. "So, other than lobbing fireballs at airheads—"

A snort interrupted him.

He ignored Zephyr. "I can heat things up a little. It's really an aspect of my other ability, and I can't do as much as my sister can. She's a heater. I'm actually still learning to control this ability."

He walked over to the cabinet and pulled out a white pillar candle on a small, silver plate, a lighter, and a hunk of metal that didn't seem to have any identity. He set them on the floor, lit the candle, then gathered the flame in his hand. Holding his hand upside down over the hunk of metal, the flame engulfed it.

Ash moved his hands, the movements almost mimicking the ones River had made earlier. The flame surrounding the metal seemed to dance to his movements. The fire flashed, flaring out suddenly and rising high.

Ash fell back on his ass, eyes wide, frantically moving his hands as if trying to suppress the flames now arcing through the air toward the door.

"He can also transform inanimate objects with fire." a deep voice said from the doorway.

We all looked in that direction, and I squeaked in surprise. A tall, well-built man with brown hair and eyes stood in the doorway, a grin on his handsome face, and a flame dancing in his outstretched hand.

"Dad!" Ash practically whined it as he picked himself up, face flushed as bright a red as the flames.

"Hey, kiddo." His dad grinned, then waggled his eyebrows as he snuffed out the flame he held. "Are you going to introduce me to the pretty little thing you're trying to impress?"

Ash's flush brightened at his dad's words. "Baby,

this is my dad, Michael Phoenix. Dad, this is Raegan."

Michael's eyebrows rose at the nickname, though he didn't say anything. "Lovely to meet you, dear."

"Not that I mind or anything," Ash said quickly, attempting to head off any questions. "But what are you doing here?"

"I'd love to say I'm just here to annoy you, but it's about the phone call you made a couple weeks ago." Michael glanced at me.

I didn't know what he was referring to, and I got the impression he was unsure of how much to say in front of me.

"It's okay, Dad," Ash assured him. "She's the one we called about."

"Well, did you find information on that myth you were talking about?" Tarin asked as he made his way over to Ash and his dad.

I stayed where I was, watching everything and hoping they'd forget I was there. This felt important, and I didn't want to be asked to leave.

Michael nodded. "It took some time, but I finally got a hold of Maybelle. She wouldn't tell me anything. She wants everyone at the Washington house in two hours. Raegan's parents included. All parents included, as a matter of fact. River, I've already talked to Serena."

"So, Mammy's in town?" Tarin asked in surprise.

"Yeah. I guess whatever is going on is major." A grim note filled Michael's voice. "She said she needed to meet with everyone, because this is going to be complicated."

"Well, baby." Ash turned to look at me. "Looks like you get to meet all the parents today."

CHAPTER FIFTEEN

RAEGAN

I trembled with nerves as I sat between Ash and Tarin in the back of the SUV.

I'd rested my head on Ash's shoulder, hoping to make the guys think I relaxed on the trip. The hands I clasped tightly between my knees told a different story. I still struggled with moving in with the guys, and now, I was going to meet their families.

Ash's hand reached around and began gently stroking my hair. It should have been awkward considering he'd used the arm I wasn't leaning on, so it stretched in front of my face. The soft strokes were calming though, and I let myself be lulled into a worry-free stupor.

It didn't take long before we'd pulled in front of a rather lovely, gray, two-story home. Several cars were parked in front, including a truck that matched Tarin's.

I swallowed hard as I climbed out of the Bronco behind Ash. Part of me wanted to grab onto a hand for reassurance, but I didn't know whose hand I wanted most.

While the house was lovely, the landscaping took my breath away. Large flower beds, with stone decorations of animals, surrounded a small pond with a fountain in the center. Ripples broke the surface. Were there fish in it? The flowers appeared to make a pattern of sorts, but I couldn't figure out the design. As we walked up to the porch, I glimpsed a vegetable garden on the side of the house.

When Tarin opened the door and walked in without knocking, I had to hold in my surprise, until I remembered it was his parents' house.

I froze just inside the foyer, unsure of what to do.

"Riva!" A tiny bundle of energy with light brown hair and a button nose launched herself at River.

My eyes widened as he reached down and scooped up the little girl, who looked so much like him. Was this the little sister he'd mentioned?

"Bethany Marie! Let your brother get in the door!"

At the shout, my head swiveled around, probably looking like something from the exorcist.

A woman walked toward us, having come from one of the side rooms. She was short, with the same light brown hair as the little girl and River, kind eyes, and wearing scrubs with dancing cupcakes.

The little girl, Bethany, leaned back until she was nearly upside down, still clutching tightly to River. "Lookie, Momma! Riva!"

"Yes, honey, I see that," she said patiently. "Now, please straighten up before you fall and break open your head."

Bethany straightened with a pout as the woman reached River and pried her daughter off him before kissing his cheek.

"Hello, honey," she said, placing Bethany on her feet.

The little cherub looked around, noticed me, and tilted her head to the side. "Who are you?"

I drew in a breath and squatted so I was on her level. "My name is Rae." I held out a hand to Bethany. "I'm a friend of your brother's."

Bethany studied me intently for a moment, then took my outstretched hand. "You're very pretty. Do you love Riva? Riva loves me, and Riva loves mommy. Does Riva love you?"

River gave a chuckle. "Okay, Bethie, why don't you go play, huh?"

He patted her and gave her a gentle push toward the other room.

She skipped off, leaving me to meet River's mother.

River straightened. "Rae, this is my mom, Serena Sage."

"It's lovely to meet you, ma'am." I held out a hand that Serena took. "Will your husband be joining us?"

The question seemed innocent until a pained look crossed Serena's lovely features.

River placed a hand on her arm. "My stepdad died before Bethie was born."

My eyes widened. "Oh my gosh, I'm so sorry."

Fuck. Of course. I couldn't afford another misstep like that. Maybe I should be a little more background today.

"It's okay, dear," Serena reassured me despite the pain on her face.

I wrapped my arms around my middle and stared at the floor. Dark hardwood gleamed under my feet, extending to the stairs at the back of the foyer. The walls were a soft, pale green, and it made an interesting contrast where they met.

A rumbling started, then several pairs of shoes

showed up in my vision. I glanced up to find three girls, all staring at me. Two appeared to be teenagers, though one was maybe closer to preteen, while I guessed the youngest to be seven or eight

"Criminy, brats." Tarin walked over to them. "I know Mom taught you manners. Stop staring."

The girls all possessed the same creamy mocha skin that I so loved on Tarin and the same dark eyes. The middle girl, though, had dark blond curls, while the other two shared Tarin's darker locks.

"Girls, you will have quite enough time to get to know her. Let the girl in the house for element's sake."

Swallowing hard at the commanding voice that echoed through the foyer, I dug my nails into my palms to still my trembling.

As heels clicked across the hardwood floors, I involuntarily backed away, ending up against Ash's chest.

Without a word, he put a hand on the small of my back, his large, warm hand brushing against the bare strip of my skin where my shirt met my jeans. Something about the touch calmed me.

The woman who entered was far from the imposing matriarch I'd expected. First of all, she was tiny, no taller than my own five feet, and possibly an inch or so shorter, if I wasn't mistaken. Her body had the softness and roundness that often came with age. It was the sparkle in her dark eyes, the happy crinkles at the corners of them, the wide, friendly smile, and the wild, barely styled, steel gray hair sticking straight out from her head that stilled what remained of my fears.

It seemed impossible to look at her and not smile. Indeed, even as I glanced back to where Tarin stood with his sisters, I noticed they were all grinning.

"Yes, Mammy," the girls all chimed as they wandered off, the youngest glancing back at me and waving.

I couldn't resist waving back.

The woman watched as the girls left, then turned to me. She strode closer, her smile wide and comforting as she reached out and took my hands with her own much smaller ones.

"Well, Let's have a look at you." She pulled me away from Ash, and for a moment, I mourned the loss of his touch. "So very pretty. Raegan, right? I'm Maybelle, Tarin's grandmother and one of the Sages, who are leaders in Elementum society." She pressed a kiss to my cheek, released my hands, then led the way into another room.

The gleaming wood floors and soft green walls

continued into the dining room. The dark, nearly black table was one of those long, rounded ones that I often thought looked like Easter eggs, the chairs matching. A long cabinet in the same nearly black color was set against one wall. A glass-fronted china cabinet was set against another wall. The only spot of color in the room, other than the soft green walls, were the crimson cushions on the chairs, and the silver candlesticks in the center of the table.

"I know it's a bit stuffy," said a deep male voice from an arched entryway on the other side of the room.

I glanced up to find a slender, blond-haired older man leaning against the arch.

"It's all family stuff, though, and my folks would freak if it wasn't here when they visit. We only use this room for meetings." The guy strode forward and held out a hand. "Kent Washington, Tarin's dad."

I took his hand while glancing between him and Tarin, who'd entered the room right behind me. This was his dad? But he looked nothing like Tarin.

"Maybe we should get the point of this meeting started, then we can have social hour," a new voice chimed in.

My head was spinning. Too many new people. Too many people, period. It was overwhelming.

The new woman was tall and statuesque. She was a large woman and carried it with a grace and elegance that seemed to dare others to say she wasn't dainty. She was also obviously Tarin's mother since she walked over and planted a kiss on his dad that left me blushing. The woman's eyes roamed the room before landing on me.

Her chin lifted, and her gaze ran over me.

I straightened, clasping my hands behind my back so the woman couldn't see me nervously playing with them. I swore she peered deep into my heart and found it lacking.

"So, this is the troublemaker?" Disapproval dripped heavily from her voice, and I shook.

I didn't mean to cause trouble. My eyes darted around the room, desperately seeking reassurance.

Tarin caught my gaze and smiled before rolling his eyes at the woman. "C'mon, Mom."

For a moment, I was certain that his mom would lose it. Then, a huge grin broke over her face, and the arms she'd crossed over her chest fell.

"I'm sorry, Tar, honey. I couldn't resist." She turned to me. "I'm Latrice, Tarin's mom. Why don't we all have a seat? We have quite a lot to talk about."

Everyone grabbed a seat around the huge table, but I hung back. They all seemed to know each other, seemed so comfortable around each other, and I couldn't help but feel like I didn't belong here. They chatted and laughed as they sat down. Even Ash's dad, Michael, and a woman he introduced as his fiancé, Kelly, were there.

An older gentleman that I'd yet to be introduced to was just sitting when the doorbell rang again.

Latrice rose to answer it, and a moment later I was delighted to see my parents and Devin come in. My parents smiled at me as they sat while Devin came over and wrapped an arm around my shoulders.

"Hey, you okay?" he whispered the question in my ear.

"Better," I whispered back, "now that you, Mom, and Dad are here."

It was true. The second I'd seen my folks and Devin, the feeling of not belonging disappeared.

Devin guided me to a seat at the table.

Why did Maybelle insist on having the families here, and what did it have to do with me?

Quiet descended slowly as everyone noticed Maybelle was standing at the head of the table, waiting.

When silence finally prevailed, Maybelle began. "Summertime has always been when the Sages travel to meet with each of the Praefectus and check in with them. We can be difficult to get a hold of. So, you can imagine my surprise when I received a rather urgent message from Michael. I know our young Rae and her family will have questions, but please give me a chance to talk first. Some of your questions may end up answered."

I clutched tighter to Devin's hand and slid against his side. I didn't want to be here, didn't want any part of whatever was going on. As much as I'd come to care for them all, I didn't belong here. I wasn't like them. No matter what they thought, I wasn't special. I just wanted to enjoy what was left of my summer before college started. I wanted to figure out what to do about my feelings for the guys and get used to the idea of not living with my parents.

I just wanted my normal back.

"When the message reached me, I was a bit surprised," Maybelle continued, unaware of my inner turmoil. "It took a little time to reach the Concilium to be sure of my knowledge, or I would have been here sooner. Some of you know, but most of you don't, so I will start at the beginning. When the boys first met Rae, they were rather surprised when Iunctura occurred without a Foederis."

An audible gasp went up from the group around

the table, and I really wished I knew what Maybelle was talking about.

"Answers were needed, and those answers are why I have brought you all here today," she continued. "We are dealing with something so rare that it has become little more than a myth in our society. Everyone knows the four Elementum: Aqua, Ignis, Terra, and Venti. What few beyond the Archivists know is that there are actually five types of Elementum. Aqua, Ignis, Terra, and Venti are all extremely common. They make up nearly the whole of our society. The Quintus, the fifth, is incredibly rare. The last one was an old man when I met him, and I was a mere child of six. Few knew of him. Even in our society, he was largely kept a secret. I only got the opportunity because he was a close friend of my Great-Uncle. He, and our Raegan here, are Spiritum. Their element is that of the Spirit."

"Spiritum?"

"What?"

"What is…?"

"How can that..?"

Everyone began talking at once.

The cacophony grew until it seemed to fill the small room.

I clamped my hands over my ears and buried my

face against Devin's chest. It was all too much. I didn't understand any of it. There were too many people. Too many words I didn't understand. What was all this? I had to be dreaming.

A hand stroked my hair, while a soft humming broke through my panic, the familiar tune calming me. Devin rocked me slightly as the tears finally dried up, and I lowered my hands.

Only then did I notice the total silence.

Embarrassed at my childish behavior, I stiffened and slid off Devin into the chair next to Tarin.

"Are you okay, dear?" Maybelle asked in a quiet voice.

"Y-yes," I stumbled over the words. "I'm s-sorry."

"It's quite all right," she said kindly. "A lot has happened to you. I'm sure it's overwhelming."

I simply nodded. It was hard to argue with the truth.

Maybelle continued to tell us about the most popular myths, debunked them, and gave us what was known of the Quintus's history. It seemed little was actually known to be fact, though. A Quintus was so rare that their own Genus often sought to hide them from even Elementum society. It seemed all the training, and all the help I would need to navigate my powers, would be found through trial and error.

Of course, first we needed to figure out what my powers were.

"I found a few things in the Tabularium, with help, of course." Maybelle gave me an apologetic look. "Still, there doesn't appear to be any consistency regarding the actual powers of the Quintus. Unlike the other Elementum, the Quintus doesn't have a physical thing to manipulate. By definition, the Quintus is the spirit, the heart, of all the Elementum. We have no way of knowing what powers our Raegan has."

"That's just it," I spoke up for the first time since my little breakdown. "I don't have powers. I've seen what the guys can do, and I've never done anything like that. Are you sure there isn't some mistake?"

At the shake of Maybelle's head, I felt acceptance finally settle inside. The fact this woman who knew so much, held such power, could be so sure spoke volumes to me.

"Simply by its nature, your power will be subtler than theirs," she explained. "It may be harder to find, and harder to control. It may be more tightly interwoven into your emotions than most Elementum. We just don't know, and for that, I'm sorry. You and the boys will be largely on your own in this. I'm afraid that my next bit of news will not make things any easier."

As Maybelle paused, Tarin's mother rose without a word and passed cups around before placing a tray of snacks in the center of the table.

I watched the others, astonished to see the seamless way that everyone worked together, passing around plates and getting drinks. Only that morning, I'd watched in fascination as the guys had seamlessly worked the same way.

"Are they a Genus?" I asked Tarin quietly.

"No, Sunshine." His response took me by surprise. "My folks are both Menda. Even though their parents are Elementum, they don't have any powers. It happens sometimes."

That caused more questions to come to mind, and I picked one at random. "Does Ash's dad have a Genus?"

"Yeah," Ash answered this time. "You'll meet them in time. We all live together right now, and most Genus do at first. As they get married and start families and stuff, they move. We don't need to be on top of each other to be a Genus."

I frowned. His explanation didn't really help.

A soft chuckle from Tarin had me shooting a glare at him.

"You'll understand eventually, Sunshine," he assured me. "Can you trust us?"

My breath caught. Did I trust them? At that moment, it hit me that I did. I trusted them with absolute certainty, even Zephyr, who scowled at me from across the table.

As I nodded, everyone settled.

Maybelle took back control of the room. "One reason it took so long to get back to you all is that we were investigating some rather disturbing rumors. We now have proof of an underground movement, and we suspect they may have had connections to Chester."

The name meant nothing to me, but Ash, his father, and his father's fiancée all stiffened.

When Michael opened his mouth, Maybelle held up a hand. "We aren't saying he survived the crash. There's no proof of that, but we are watching carefully. Our bigger concern is that they may come after Raegan, if they know about her."

"They know," Z said, voice flat.

"Are you sure?" Tarin's dad asked.

I expected Z to answer, but Devin spoke up instead. "They've already tried to kidnap her. Three times."

"I think I need...a minute." I didn't know if

anyone heard the words that barely left my mouth, and I didn't care as I stood and left the room.

I didn't want any of the guys to join me, either. I needed a moment to come to grips with everything. Accepting that I was the Quintus meant accepting that I was also being hunted, simply for existing.

It wasn't just my life in danger, though. As long as the guys were my Genus, as long as they stood with me, they were in danger, too.

I leaned on the wall by the dining room, letting it all sink in.

How could I do this? How could I put their lives in danger? I knew the answer, though. Trust. I'd seen what they could do. I needed to trust them and their abilities.

Closing my eyes, I took a deep, bracing breath. I could do this.

As I pushed away from the wall, Maybelle's voice drifting out of the dining room stopped me. "I'm glad Rae needed a moment. There's something we should address, and I don't wish to overwhelm her further."

Part of me wanted to cover my ears because I didn't know how much more I could handle right now. A lot was getting thrown at me, a lifetime's worth in reality. I also suspected that if I walked back in there right now, the discussion would stop.

No matter how overwhelming all this was, I wanted all the info I could get.

"The nature of a Genus, of the bond created, is intense and unique," Maybelle continued.

"What do you mean?" Mom asked.

I wanted to peek in, but I didn't dare.

For a moment, no one spoke, then Michael said, "This is my daughter and her Genus."

"So, it's not unusual for a Genus to be mixed gender?" Mom asked in confusion.

"Not at all. But that's not really the point of the picture." Michael paused again briefly. "The three men are also all my daughter's boyfriends. These two are also dating each other."

"And now you understand my concern." Heaviness filled Maybelle's words. "And the reason for calling everyone together. Not everyone can handle a polyamorous relationship. We've had Genus so strained by infighting that they were useless. We've even had a few that were so strained it caused Foederis, a breaking of the Iunctura bond. Rae is the first Spiritum born in over a hundred years. The one I met died shortly after, and he was well on in years. Before him, it had been so long since one was born that we have no real record, only stories. We can't even be sure that any of them were true. Spiritum are rare and powerful, and it seems someone wants yours. You cannot afford to be fighting, not now. If any of you have feelings for Rae, you need to talk about them. You need to find a way to make a polyamorous relationship work if more than one of you has feelings for her. And part of making it work is having the right support."

"This is a lot to take in." I shifted at Mom's voice. "This sort of thing ain't normal. More than one guy dating our daughter?"

"Sweetheart, I'm pretty sure we abandoned normal when the wild-haired guy disappeared from our living room and left a white-haired infant behind." Bless my dad for always being the voice of reason.

Mom sighed. "I suppose you're right. It's gonna take some getting used to."

As the others chimed in with agreement, I sat back against the wall again, my mind reeling.

I could be with them all? It seemed too good to be true. It wouldn't be easy, though. Ash and Tarin seemed at odds, Z didn't seem to like me, and I couldn't quite put a finger on River, yet.

Could we really be together that way? I wanted to try, but how would the guys feel about it? I'd wait until they came to me. Even if I wanted this,

Maybelle was right. They couldn't afford to be fighting. If I thought being together was hurting their Genus, I'd pull the plug. I refused to come between them.

My decision made and my resolve strong, I straightened. I couldn't be the pouty, panicky, overwhelmed child anymore. If I wanted to make this unusual relationship work, I needed to be strong. If I wanted to keep myself and the guys safe, I would need to be smart and trained. I needed to pull myself together and become a better, stronger version of myself. A version who would be worthy of being with the incredible guys gifted to me.

I strode back into the dining room, a new confidence and surety settling on my shoulders. Needing his calm, I made my way to where River sat.

He smiled as he saw me and pushed his chair away from the table enough for me to settle in his lap.

"I'm sorry. I'm okay now." I smiled at everyone.

"It's all right. I think that's enough for now," Maybelle said.

The sharp sound of hands being clapped together made me jump in River's lap.

He chuckled, and I shot him a glare.

Everyone swiveled their gazes to Tarin's mom. "Since everyone is here, why don't we make a party of it? It would give everyone a chance to catch up and get to know Rae and her family."

Those seemed to be magic words because kids came pouring in and chaos ensued.

Perfectly content in River's arms, I burrowed a bit and took in the mayhem. I still felt overwhelmed and nervous, but I could handle it.

After all, I had four wonderful guys standing by my side.

CHAPTER SIXTEEN

RAEGAN

W hile the discussion didn't stop with Tarin's mom's words, it became more informal. My parents wanted to know more about the Elementum world, and everyone speculated on my powers.

I wanted to bury myself against River's chest for a while. I'd never been shy, but the number of people in the house made me retreat inside myself.

When Tarin's sisters came over and pulled me out of River's lap, it became obvious retreating wouldn't happen.

After dragging me to the living room, the girls shoved me onto the couch. They plopped around me, the older two on either side, pulling their legs up and crossing them so they could sit facing me, and the younger of the three climbed onto her eldest sister's lap.

"Okay, spill. Which one do you like best?" asked the oldest, skipping straight past the formality of introductions to get to the gossip.

My chest felt tight at the sudden, unexpected question.

"It's got to be Ash, right?" The middle one's eyes glazed over as they drifted around the room to find Ash, and a soft sigh escaped her.

Giggles erupted from my other side.

"Farrah has a huge crush on Ash," the youngest one gleefully informed me, bouncing in her sister's lap and clapping her hands.

Farrah's head whipped around, and she speared her sister with a glare, a flush of red creeping up her cheeks. "I do not, Aurae! You're such a brat."

The oldest rolled her eyes. "Oh, come on. You totally do. Everyone knows it. Pretty sure Ash knows it, too. And you know nothing will happen. Ash is practically a second brother to us. He grew up with us, for Element's sake!"

I didn't stop the giggle from escaping. "Is this what having sisters is like?"

"Oh, Elements, I'm sorry. Too much? I should have reigned them in." The oldest shot her sisters a glare. "We're just a little excited. You're the first girl Tarin's ever brought home, and it's obvious he likes you. Since you're part of their Genus, it's like getting a whole new sister."

"I...um...It's okay, but do I have to choose a favorite?" I picked at my jeans, gaze firmly planted on the floor in front of the couch.

"Elements, no!" the oldest girl laughed.

"Mckenna's motto is Why Choose," Aurae piped up, tugging at one of her curly blond pigtails.

The oldest, Mckenna, batted her hand away and fixed the girl's half-undone hair as color seeped into her cheeks. "Ignore her. It's just a phrase from my online book club. We aren't fans of love triangles in books and find it frustrating that the girl always has to choose and one great guy gets left alone."

I'd never thought about that before, but she was right. Why should one great guy always get left behind? Since I couldn't comment on that, I searched my brain for something else to talk about. I wanted to get to know Tarin's sister. Really, I wanted to know all the guys' families. I just didn't know where to start.

Then, I realized I'd been handed a ready-made source of information.

"So, are you guys all earth elementals, too?" I

figured I'd start with something easy since I knew nothing about this new world I'd been thrust into.

"Terra."

I wasn't sure which of the girls spoke up. "What?"

"It's Terra," Mckenna corrected. "Not Earth. And Elementum, not Elemental." She smiled, softening any harshness I might feel. "There are going to be a lot of new terms for you to learn. It's normal to forget or stumble. We all went through it. To answer your question, no. Except for Aurae. She's Ventus."

I struggled to remember the terms the guys used only that morning. "Um...Air?"

Little Aurae beamed, nodded, then held out her open palm, face up. She twirled the fingers of her other hand over the open palm and a very tiny whirlwind formed. "That's all I can do right now, but I'm learning."

I smiled at her obvious pride and delight. "I can't do anything yet, so you got me beat. So, um, how come she's the only one?" I cringed as the words came out all wrong.

I hoped I hadn't offended them.

"Our parents are Menda," Farrah said.

I turned my head to see her better.

"That means they were born to Elementum parents, but hold no Elementum powers themselves," she explained. "That two of their four children attained abilities is pretty amazing. There's only like a twenty-five percent chance of a Menda pairing having a powered child."

"Oh." I didn't know what else to say.

My questions seemed silly now. There appeared to be a lot more to my new world than I thought. I'd stepped on enough toes for one day.

"Girls." The musical tone of River's mother, Serena, washed over me. "Why don't you give Raegan a little space?"

The girls grinned and scattered without a complaint.

Serena sat down on the couch, a mug in one hand, steam curling from it.

"So, are you an Elementum?" I asked, my curiosity overriding any common sense.

Serena shook her head. "No. I'm just human. River's father and stepfather were Aqua, though."

Serena gestured to where River and Zephyr wrestled on the floor like a couple of eight-year-olds instead of grown men with jobs.

I smiled at their playfulness. It was the first time I'd seen Zephyr so relaxed. Hearing a deep, contented sigh next to me, I glanced over to find River's mom smiling at them, a dreamy expression on her face.

"I'm so happy Zephyr found them," she said.

I cocked my head to the side, and River's mom chuckled softly.

"The guys are all close. I guess being part of a Genus does that to you, but River and Zephyr share a unique connection. It sometimes makes me wish his brother—" She stopped abruptly, her eyes widening as her grip on the brightly colored coffee mug tightened.

"His brother?" I asked in confusion. "But I thought—"

River's mom cut my words off with a frantic shake of her head, rose from the couch, and headed into the kitchen.

Since the invitation was obvious, I leaped up to follow.

The kitchen made me drool. Granite counters, stainless steel appliances, gleaming wood cabinets, a large pot rack with all manner of cookware hanging from it, all of it straight out of my dreams.

I enjoyed cooking, and in a kitchen like this, it would be nothing less than pure pleasure.

Serena settled heavily into one of the chairs at the small table. She set down her mug and rested her head in her hands.

I settled near her, waiting patiently.

Serena drew in a deep, shaky breath and raised her head to look at me with a wry smile. "We don't talk about it, and honestly, I don't know how much River remembers since he was so little."

She seemed like she'd been transported away from the kitchen, and a glistening wetness in her eyes betrayed her feelings. The heaviness in her voice told me whatever she needed to say would be difficult for her. I rested a hand on Serena's to offer comfort and strength.

"I met River's father the day I turned eighteen. He was older, in his early twenties, gorgeous, sophisticated, and exuded power. I was flattered that he wanted to spend time with me." She pushed back her light brown hair as she finally met my eyes. "I was young, and I fell too hard, too fast. I believed it was the same for him, too. While my parents didn't like it, they couldn't do much to stop us. Before long, I moved in with him."

The pain on her face was more than I could take, and I reached out an arm to hug her around the shoulders.

Serena leaned into me as she continued, "A few months later, I was getting sick all the time, and he was the one who suggested a pregnancy test. It hadn't even crossed my mind that I could be pregnant. I freaked out, but he was so calm. We started talking about getting married, and I could just stay home and take care of the baby. For a bit, I was walking on air. I was going to get my happily ever after at eighteen. Who gets that lucky?"

For a minute her face shone at the memory, and I saw a glimpse of the eighteen-year-old beauty she must have been, the beauty that her son inherited.

She rose and carried her mug to the sink, rinsing it out and putting it back in the cupboard. "No one," a sob escaped as she spoke. "No one gets that lucky."

When she returned to the table, she had contained her tears, and she sank heavily into her chair. "When the time came, I had twin boys, River and Raine. For a couple of years, we were happy. And then, fate kicked us in the ass. I had gone back to work, and the boys were in daycare. River got really sick one day, and I stayed home, but we sent Raine to daycare so I could focus on River. Their father picked him up on his way home from work, but they never made it." Her voice cracked.

Not needing her to continue to guess what happened next, I shook my head.

She continued, anyway. "The guy was so drunk, they said it was a miracle he drove as far as he did before hitting someone. Raine was three and a half."

Damn. How could River remember any of that? Did he often feel like something was missing? I'd heard something like that about twins once.

"He seemed to withdraw a bit after that. He'd always been the more vivacious of the pair. After a while, he had Ash and Tarin, and the three have always been close. But when Zephyr came onto the scene… I don't know, it was like he became that little boy again. There's just something special between him and Zephyr." Serena drew in a deep breath and shook herself. "I'm sorry. I didn't mean to burden you with my sob story. It's just the only way to explain why his relationship with Zephyr means so much to me." She smiled and stood. "We should rejoin the others."

My mind reeled. River had a twin brother that he lost so young. His connection to the others must be even more important than even he realized.

As we walked back into the room, the first thing to hit me was the quiet. With a glance around, I noticed Zephyr sitting cross-legged on the floor in front of little Aurae.

Curious, I stepped closer, my head cocked to one side like a puppy. A soft smile drifted onto my face as I watched Z patiently teaching Aurae about her powers. His gentleness revealed a side of the grumpy bear I'd not witnessed to that point.

Z spoke softly, positioning Aurae's fingers and moving her through motions, then he did the same thing with his hands in slow motion.

The hint of a tiny, pink tongue poked from between Aurae's lips as she concentrated on Z's fingers.

Utterly fascinated by Z's gentleness, I moved closer until I could just hear their soft voices.

"Okay, ready?" Z asked. "One...Two...Three."

At the same time, both Z and Aurae made the motions, and I watched as little whirlwinds appeared on their open palms, then began to grow and shrink, almost like an exaggerated pulsing.

Aurae's face lit up as her little whirlwind pulsed in time with Z's.

A hand on my arm made me jump.

"Sorry, dear." The gentle voice of Tarin's grandmother, Maybelle, washed away my jumpiness. "How are you holding up? I know this is quite a lot to take in. Zephyr didn't have the easiest time of it when he joined us two years ago."

Maybelle exuded calm and confidence, while at the same time, she didn't put off the usual grandmother vibes. She just seemed like a much older, more experienced friend.

Perhaps that was what made me speak up.

"Actually, I do have a question." I licked my lips, and my eyes darted around the room, searching for the boys. I dropped my voice to a mere whisper when I went on. "It's about, um, Iunctura." I hesitated, unsure how to ask what I needed to know.

Maybelle patted my arm and smiled at me. "It's okay, just spit it out."

"Okay. So, um, the bond, Iunctura," I said, the unfamiliar word feeling odd in my mouth. "It makes connections, right? Like, special connections?" Oh God, I was rambling. "Does it, um, create emotions? Like, can it create attractions?"

I felt my face flame as I finally got the words out.

"Oh, Elements, no!" Maybelle chuckled. "My dear, free will is something that can never be taken away from us. If you're attracted to any or even all of them, that's your own heart's choice, not some bond forcing feelings on you."

A weight lifted from my shoulders that had been there since hearing about Iunctura. I'd feared what it meant for my feelings, my heart.

"Iunctura may cause the feelings to advance faster than they might normally do. You'll certainly be far more passionate and feel your love far deeper than others will," she continued. "The last Quintus was attracted to men. But while his Genus were all men, only two of them were also attracted men. To hear him tell it, he had quite the passionate affair with the ones who shared his desires, and a bond deeper than family with the other two."

I understood where she was going with this. Even if I might develop feelings for all the guys, that didn't mean we all had to date to still have a solid Genus, so long as we all valued and respected each other.

Maybelle squeezed my arm in reassurance. "Iunctura strengthens what's in your heart. It can't create something from nothing. Your feelings are and always will be your own."

With my main concern settled, I still had a couple of questions. "What does Quintus mean?"

"It's a slang term, really, for what you are. Quintus, meaning fifth element," she explained. "The actual term for your element is Spiritum."

That didn't really explain what I was, but I was beginning to understand it was because no one really knew. "I just have one more question."

She dipped her head. "You can ask anything, dear."

"How did the others know Iunctura had happened?" This had been bothering me since learning that was how Genus recognized each other. "How did they know I was part of their Genus?"

Sympathy filled Maybelle eyes. "Usually, Elementum feel Iunctura as soon as they are close to each other, but according to the last Quintus, Spiritum don't feel the bond form. But I can assure you that the Iunctura between you and the boys is solid, and it grows stronger with every second."

"I'm not sure whether to be relieved or disappointed," I said with a wry grin. "Although honestly, I'm more overwhelmed and exhausted than anything else."

"It's understandable. You've been through a great deal. Give me your phone." Maybelle held out a hand.

My curiosity piqued; I gave her my phone.

"I'm adding my number, just in case you have questions. I'm not supposed to have my phone on official business, but I do, anyway. Until recently, I was listed as the guardian to a minor, so it's a habit to have it on me. Anytime, day or night, leave a message, and I'll get back to you. Never be afraid to reach out. There are no stupid questions." Maybelle handed my phone back to me, giving my hair a gentle stroke as she called out, "Boys, I think it's time to take your girl home. She's exhausted."

Ash practically flew to my side, picking me up

and kissing my forehead. "You okay, baby? Ready to go?"

I simply nodded, leaning into Ash's embrace as the others joined us. I hadn't realized exactly how tired I felt.

Around me, I heard the sounds of the others making their goodbyes as my eyes drifted shut and exhaustion took over.

CHAPTER SEVENTEEN

ZEPHYR

Water rose from the bucket set to the side and speared toward me in a spiral.

Thrusting my hands out, I directed the air around me in a concentrated stream. It knocked most of the water torpedo off course, but some still splashed my face.

A giggle came from the side of the practice mat, and I shot a glare at the menace sitting on the floor with Ash and Tarin, who hovered around her like a pair of love-struck idiots.

Fucking hell. I hated how that slip of a woman turned those two inside out. I still didn't trust her, which wasn't exactly a secret.

Pale gray eyes met mine, and the giggle died. When her smile fell, my stomach dropped.

Dammit. I didn't mean to make her feel bad; it's just that this whole damn thing with a fifth element felt like so much bullshit.

"You need to give her a chance," River muttered as he threw a fist forward.

I dodged the stream of water and the fist, whipped my hand around to gather the air near River's ankles, and tugged. We were supposed to be limiting our powers since we still didn't know if Raegan would have an active power or not, but using them was second nature.

River hit the mat with a thud and popped back to his feet right away. "Come on, she's actually pretty cool if you spend time with her."

I rolled my eyes and didn't respond as I continued to dodge and attack. I refused to waste my breath saying the same things I'd been saying since that girl tumbled into our lives.

Again, I glanced at where she sat between Tarin and Ash, the pair of them finding ways to touch her or get her attention.

Idiots. I couldn't figure out if Tarin was genuinely interested in the girl, if it was competitive, or if there was something else going on.

None of this made any sense. Not the way they were both acting, not Ash's immediate crush, not the whole fifth element thing.

Of course, I was still figuring things out. I didn't grow up in this world, not like Tarin, Ash, and River. It took a long time for River to get through to me when we met. Why would he assume anything would be different with this girl?

"Come on, Zephyr," River cajoled. "She's here, and she ain't going anywhere. You can't avoid her forever."

Fuck. He was right, and I didn't like it.

I threw another punch, followed by an elbow to the ribs.

"Oof." River shook his head as the elbow caught him by surprise, landing harder than I intended.

Stepping back, I gave him a minute, then let my annoyance drive my hits and kicks as we continued to spar.

This time, River didn't let up on his efforts to talk up the girl. His words became a drone, an annoying buzz in my ear. I wasn't changing my mind until I knew more. There were exactly four people in the world I trusted, and three of them were in this room. The girl was an unknown factor, and according to what we were told, she shouldn't even exist.

The more River talked, the more annoyed I got, and the more reckless my hits and kicks became. Sweat rolled down my face, and even River breathed hard and quit talking.

Gasps and murmurs came from our audience the harder and longer we fought.

River pushed away from me, grabbed my wrists, spun me around, and held me against him as he whispered in my ear. "She's ours now. She belongs with us. Get over yourself."

With a twist and a shove, I broke his hold. Did he have any idea how much of an asshole he sounded like when he said that?

I stared at him a moment before rushing in, blindly throwing punches.

How could he talk like that?

"She doesn't belong to anyone," I said as River blocked every punch I threw. "I don't need to like her immediately."

Fire burned in my belly as I fought harder while River calmed the more I came at him. "You need to act like you at least accept she's one of us. This is hard enough for her."

My chest tightened as the fire burned hotter. Hard for her? River knew more than the others. He knew the things I'd been through. Hard for her? Did none of them think about how this would be for me? They'd barely asked my opinion on anything concerning the girl, and now, they expected me to fall at her feet?

River flowed around me like the body of water he was named for. With every punch I threw, he was suddenly not there. The more he evaded me, the hotter my ire burned, especially because he didn't stop trying to talk up the girl.

For Element's sake!

"Will you just stop!" I hissed when we closed the distance again.

Grabbing the back of his neck, I pulled our foreheads together, forcing him to stop and see how serious I was. I would come to whatever place I'd land with the girl in my own time. They needed to drop this shit.

"I don't need to be falling all over the girl like the rest of you," I seethed. "She isn't going anywhere."

"Then, at least, stop being an ass." River pulled from my grip.

Fury filled me. I wasn't being an ass. I was being me. Why did I need to make nice because some girl made doe eyes at these idiots?

I threw punches blindly, not caring if they landed. I needed to work this anger out of me. If River fought back, I didn't feel it. Not until a spear of ice hit me square in the chest.

Unprepared for the force of the strike, I fell back. A resounding thud echoed through the room as my head impacted the mat.

Shouting and running feet filled the air as I sat up and shook my head.

Facing me, River knelt on the mat, breath heaving, blood running down his face from his nose and one eye beginning to swell. Tarin ran fingers over his face, gently prodding, while Ash crouched between us.

I'd done that to him? We pulled our punches when we sparred, but I'd been super pissed.

Fuck. While I might not appreciate his actions, I didn't want to hurt him.

White hair blocked my view of River abruptly as the girl dropped beside me. "Oh my God, are you okay?"

Her hand reached toward the back of my head, but I jerked to the side, trying to get a view of River again.

She frowned. "Let me look. You could have done serious damage."

Dammit, I needed to see River's expression, see

how pissed he might be. The damn girl could go coddle one of the others.

Swatting at her still-seeking hand, I scrambled to my feet. "Cut it out!"

Thank the Elements River's face remained calm as ever for the ten seconds I saw it before a cloud of white hair filled my vision.

"What the fuck is your damage?" Fire flared in her pale gray eyes. "I'm trying to help you, for fuck's sake. Maybe you could yank the stick out of your ass long enough to say thank you or something. Surely, your mother taught you manners."

Oh, I was so done with the damn girl. "My mother was too busy fucking Johns for her next hit to teach me anything except for how useless girls are."

"Look, mister." The girl poked my chest with her finger, which I swatted. "I might not know what I can do yet, but obviously, I'm needed for something, or I wouldn't be here, connected to the bunch of you."

I stepped forward into her space, forcing her to back up a bit. Malicious glee filled me when uncertainty flashed across her face. "Power or not, you aren't needed. We were fine without you. We were perfect without you. You're nothing more than an anomaly, a myth, an outdated toy that no one wants. Four Elementum make a complete Genus.

There is nothing you can bring to this family that we can't do on our own or with the help of other Elementum. You know why no one knew what you were? Because you're redundant. You aren't needed, anymore."

For a moment, tears shimmered in her eyes. Then she straightened, squared her shoulders, and stepped forward. "I wouldn't be here if I was redundant. Someone a whole lot smarter than you knew I had a purpose, that you all needed me. Either way, it doesn't matter because, from what I understand, I'm here, and I'm not going anywhere. You better get used to me being around. As for my powers, when I do figure those out and finally use them to save your ass from some fire you've landed it in, I'll be happy to accept your thanks and your apology. So, go ahead, pout about the new person in your little group and have your little tantrums." She waved a hand through the air, a smirk playing across her lips.

That smirk got to me before the silence finally registered.

I glanced up to find the others watching us avidly. River held an ice pack to his eye, face impassive, while Ash and Tarin glared at me.

Okay, sure, maybe I'd gone a bit too far, but the girl bounced right back and got in my face. My pulse raced, the blood pounding in my ears as I refocused on the angry spitfire in front of me. That smirk made me want to do something I'd regret, and the longer I stayed silent, the smirkier she got.

Fuck, I wanted to wipe that smirk off her face.

"Don't. Treat me. Like. A child." I leaned down, putting my face in hers and letting my voice drop into a threatening, growly tone. This girl needed to learn her place, and while I appreciated her nerve, she needed to get away from me. "You're just a stupid little girl pretending to know what she's talking about."

Her smirk twisted into a snarl, and she slapped my chest. "You!"

Taken aback, I stumbled a step away.

"Are an asshole!" She slapped my chest again. "And someday, someone is going to put you in your place, and I hope I'm there to watch!"

When her hand came up again, this time I grabbed her wrist and yanked her against me. "Smack me again, and I'll show you exactly what my mother taught me about what women are good for."

Pale eyes widened, her chest heaved, and every inch of the body pressed tightly against mine trembled as I held her in place. Her tongue darted out, wetting her lips before she swallowed hard.

Every muscle in my body held tense as I stared down at the slip of a girl who had invaded my life. The air around us thickened, and time nearly stopped until she was ripped from my grasp.

Ash's angry gaze filled my vision. "Cut it out."

I drew in a deep breath. Dammit, I needed some space from this girl, from everyone right now.

"I'm going out. Keep her away from me from now on." I didn't wait for a response before storming up the stairs and out the door.

CHAPTER EIGHTEEN

TARIN

I watched Zephyr storm off, stunned by the display we'd just witnessed.

What the fuck was that all about?

"I'm, um, gonna go to my room," Rae spoke so softly I barely heard her.

I wanted to stop her, hug her, comfort her, do *something* to wipe that look off her face. But as I took a step in her direction, a hand on my arm stopped me.

When I glanced back, Ash shook his head.

He was right. We both knew how volatile girls could be. We both had sisters. Sometimes, it was best to let things sit a bit. Their argument got heated so quickly, and a lot of things were said that likely hurt.

With her gone, I sank to the mats on the floor.

Ash and River joined me, and River sighed, "Well, that was a clusterfuck."

"We have to do something about his attitude," Ash said.

"I tried." River waved a hand at the mats. "You saw how well that went."

We sat in silence for a while.

If River couldn't talk to him, neither Ash nor I had a chance of getting through to Zephyr. Of course, we should have known he'd be reluctant. When River met him, it took weeks before he did more than treat him like a customer. Getting him into our family, introduced into the world he belonged to, had taken months, and even then, he'd only begun to see Ash and me as friends, as family, after living with us for a couple months.

His reaction to Rae just seemed extreme, though.

"Did you see her face as she left?" Ash leaned forward, drawing his knees up and resting his arms on them. "She put up a good front, but his words really hurt her. Maybe we should do something to make her feel better. Take her out or something?"

I loved the idea of taking Rae on a date, but I knew that wasn't what Ash meant. At some point, I'd find time to take her out on a real date, and I knew Ash wanted to as well. I couldn't explain the friction between us when it came to Rae. Poly relationships happened with Elementum. That's just how it was.

"Maybe a movie? Dinner?" River threw out suggestions, but I shook my head.

If we wanted to cheer her up, sitting in a dark theater where her mind could wander wouldn't help. We needed something with a lot to do.

"Elemental Fallout is playing tonight." Ash held up his phone. "I could make a call."

Elemental Fallout was his sister's band, and they'd been making a splash locally. If they were playing a club, there'd be a lot of high energy, and they always put on a good show.

River and I both nodded, and Ash pushed a button.

River and I listened to his side of the conversation. "Hey, Sera. You're playing tonight, right?"

...

"Yeah, actually, that's why I was calling. We thought Rae could use a distraction."

...

"Yeah, really?"

...

"Awesome, thanks."

...

"Love you, too. Later." He hung up and turned to us. "We're all set. She's going to put us on a backstage list, too, if we want."

There were advantages to being related to a rising star, apparently. "I'll go talk to Rae." I rose and pointed to River. "You should clean up."

Dried blood still adorned his face, and his eye would soon become pretty colors.

River shot me a middle-finger salute.

The silent, still air in the house would be reminiscent of the feel of early morning if not for how heavy and tense it felt. Unease stirred in me. We needed to find some kind of happy medium with Zephyr.

The door to Rae's room was closed when I got there. I knew better than to barge in, so I tapped gently.

Her muffled reply came through. "Go away."

I needed to tread carefully, or I'd end up the subject of her ire. I'd been on that end of things before.

"Not going to happen, Sunshine." I made sure it came off as gently joking.

No reply came, but careful listening brought sounds of shifting, then soft footsteps.

The door cracked open. "I thought you were Z. I really want to be alone."

"I know, but we're worried about you." I leaned against the doorframe. "Zephyr said some harsh things down there. Of course, you threw some hard things right back. Didn't know you had it in you."

A tear rolled down her cheek. "I was a complete bitch, wasn't I? Oh God, I should apologize." Her pale gray eyes widened. "Do you think I hurt him?"

Elements, this girl was too sweet for her own good.

With a hand, I pushed the door open, then gathered her against my chest. "Sunshine, you have nothing to worry about. You were fighting back against someone being a total dick. He started on you first, and he shouldn't have if he didn't want to get it right back."

"But the things I said…" She clung to me. "Oh, God. I was horrible."

"I guarantee Zephyr isn't spending a moment worrying about your feelings right now, and he isn't spending one moment worrying about the things you said," I assured her.

Rae shook her head. "Doesn't matter. I shouldn't have said the things I did."

I held up my hands, knowing I wouldn't win this.

"Okay. Well, I also wanted to find out if you might be interested in going out tonight. You, me, River, and Ash. Elemental Fallout is playing at a local club, and Ash has an in with the band."

If possible, her eyes widened more, and her jaw dropped. "Elemental Fallout! Hell, yeah! They're awesome!"

"You know them?" It was my turn to be surprised.

They'd been making a big splash locally, but for some reason, I hadn't expected them to be Rae's speed. After all, I was pretty sure I'd heard the musical stylings of Divas coming from her room.

"Yeah, I mean, I only saw them once. Devin took us to this festival in the park, and they were playing. Not my usual style, but they're incredible. And their lead singer is sex on a stick." She shoved out of my hold and turned toward her closet. "What am I going to wear? Where are they playing? That will matter. When do we leave?"

While my arms felt empty without her in them, her excitement was infectious.

I laughed as I answered her. "In order: I don't know. A club, though Ash didn't specify which one. And, like, eight, I think. Don't want to be too early, but we have a little surprise for you beforehand."

She spun around, eyes narrowing. "What surprise?"

I shook my head at her. "If I told you, it wouldn't be a surprise."

"Humph." She stomped her foot and went back to her closet. "Fine."

When she started tossing clothes out of her closet, I left.

I didn't want any part of that.

Zephyr made himself scarce until dinner, and the minute Rae joined us, he scowled and stomped back to his room.

River frowned. "I'll make him a plate and take it up to him."

"Will he be joining us tonight?" Rae asked between mouthfuls of chicken.

River's blue eyes darted to her, then back to the ceiling. "I doubt it, but I'll ask him. Clubs aren't really his thing. Not since he stopped tending bar."

"I hate leaving him out."

River shook his head. "He won't feel left out as long as it's offered. We've gone to a couple clubs over the years as a group, but he never liked joining us."

"Okay, if you're sure." Rae finished her dinner, then shoved away from the table. "I need to get ready. I'll see you guys shortly."

Good thing we'd all showered after the sparring session. It was likely she'd be in the bathroom for a while.

I met Ash's eyes and smirked at his shocked face.

Yeah, he had a sister, but he'd only known about her for a year. He'd moved out before she'd moved in, so little things like how long a girl took to get ready to go anywhere still surprised him.

"I'll clean up if you two want to go get ready." I made the offer knowing it wouldn't take me long to throw something on.

They nodded and headed upstairs.

Taking a deep breath, I let the quiet wash over me. I enjoyed early mornings, usually, for this very reason. Our household tended to be chaotic, so moments of quiet and calm were rare. Even now, I could hear the sounds of the shower, faint strains of music, clomping of feet. Background noise that I found comforting.

The guys had left their dishes in the sink, so I rinsed them off and loaded up the dishwasher. After starting it, I wiped everything down, swept the floor, and double-checked to make sure everything was put away.

While we might not be great at keeping the clutter from piling up, we tried to make sure the space stayed clean.

With dinner dealt with, I headed to my room.

Zephyr's door was cracked, and harsh whispers reached my ears, so I peeked in to make sure everything was all right. Zephyr stood against the wall with River inches from him, one hand on the wall next to Zephyr's head. They were so intent on each other that they didn't notice me. Neither seemed upset, just intense.

Those two had the strangest relationship.

Shaking my head, I left them to each other and went to dig around in my closet.

I settled on a pair of loose, black jeans with a belt to make sure they stayed on my hips, a plain white tee under a pinstripe vest, and a pair of black, white, and red high-top sneakers.

Grabbing a couple gold chains, I tossed them on and headed to the living room to wait for the others.

As I passed the bathroom, I noticed it stood empty, so I ducked in and spritzed myself with body spray.

I wasn't at all surprised to find I was the first one ready, but Ash and River weren't far behind me.

Upon seeing River, I laughed. "We're going to a club, not the beach."

River shrugged and sank onto the couch. In his cargo shorts and white tee with a stylized wave, all he needed was a pair of flip-flops, and he'd be ready for some sun and sand.

Ash came down in a pair of torn black jeans, a fitted burgundy shirt, and his black motocross jacket. The jacket likely wouldn't make it into the club, but I figured he wanted it just in case.

Several minutes passed before we heard soft footfalls on the stairs.

When Rae entered the living room, my jaw hit the floor. In a pair of light wash, torn to hell jeans, a short, white corset top with tiny pink flowers, silver heels, and cropped leather jacket, she was a knockout. She'd piled her white hair on the crown of her head in some kind of messy bun, and while I knew she had makeup on, it was so subtle you couldn't tell.

A quick glance revealed Ash and River similarly dumbstruck.

I shook off my reaction. "You look incredible."

A blush spread over her cheeks. "Thanks."

"We should get going," Ash finally spoke. "You

are going to draw a lot of attention in that outfit. I love it."

As I followed them out, I watched the little sway in Rae's walk.

Fucking hell, this girl was going to kill me yet.

CHAPTER NINETEEN

RAEGAN

My entire body vibrated as we piled into River's SUV.

Everyone except Ash.

I paused with one foot in the backseat. "You aren't coming? Aren't you the one getting us in?"

"Don't worry, baby." Ash shot me a grin and a wink. "I don't want to crowd into the car, so I'm taking my bike." He waggled his keys. "You could join me?"

Part of me wanted to hop on his bike and see what it would be like. Devin talked about getting a bike someday, but I'm not sure he'd actually do it. The idea of flying down the road on his bike, the wind in my hair, sent my pulse racing.

But I didn't want to show up to the club and the

surprise with windblown, messy hair. "Maybe next time."

"You're missing out." He stepped closer and leaned toward me.

Holy shit. Was he about to kiss me? In front of everyone? I mean, Tarin already did, so maybe I shouldn't be surprised. Except, holy fuck.

I held my breath, but he ducked to the side and planted a kiss on my cheek, right next to my ear.

"The first time I kiss you for real, it won't be with an audience." The words ghosted over my ear, sending shivers down my spine.

He drew back, winked again, and turned to his bike.

After watching him put on his helmet and tear off down the drive, I climbed into the car.

Next to me, River grinned but said nothing.

I planned to ply Ash with questions until he cracked like a walnut about this surprise. With him on his bike, my plans needed to change.

Between River and Tarin, I thought River was more likely to crack. "Okay, I need details, right now."

"No idea what you're talking about." River's grin gave him away.

Tarin leaned forward between the front seats. "Don't you dare ruin Ash's surprise, man."

River shook his head. "I would never. I want to see her face."

"You can see my face. It's right here." I waved a hand at my face. "Now, tell me." I put a little whine in my voice, which didn't work.

River shook his head and continued to grin.

I flopped back against the seat. Whatever was going on, they weren't cracking. Excitement still coursed through me, and it warred with anticipation. I couldn't wait to see Elemental Fallout. The only thing that would make it more fun would be...

"Hey." I sat straight up and swiveled my head between River and Tarin. "Is this a thing that needs tickets or whatever? I mean, can I invite Devin and Pier?"

Tarin pulled his phone out. "I'll check with Ash, but it should be fine."

He shot off a text.

"Oh my God, no! Don't text him on his bike!" All I could see was disaster because Ash didn't strike me as the kind to wait.

Tarin leveled me with a serious stare. "Ash would never check his phone on his bike."

"Then, who are you texting?" I asked in confusion.

His phone pinged. "Someone who knows that it's okay."

He waggled his phone, and I made a grab for it, unsuccessfully. Brat, but a fucking cute one with his grin.

"Nope." He held it out of reach. "I'm not ruining Ash's surprise. We're going to Hazy Logic. Have them meet us."

Wrinkling my nose at him, I flopped back in the seat, letting it go for now. Besides, I needed to text Devin and Pier.

Raegan: Guys, get your butts to Hazy Logic. Elemental Fallout is playing. The guys are taking me, and now, you're officially on the list.

Devin: K

Pierson: o((^ ▽^*))o*

After a couple minutes passed without any more texts, I figured they must be coordinating between themselves. They'd text me when they got there. And since neither River nor Tarin would spill the beans on the surprise, there wasn't much to do except enjoy the drive.

When we pulled into the club, River pulled

around back. I frowned. "Why are we going to the back?"

"All part of the surprise." River said as he shut the car off.

When I climbed out, I spotted Ash leaning against the wall by the back door.

He sauntered over to us and grabbed my hand, tugging me to the door.

"Come on. You're gonna love this." He knocked on the door, and it cracked open.

The guy on the other side glanced at Ash, nodded, and opened the door fully.

Mind blown. No. No way we were going backstage. How the hell did he pull this off?

Pretty sure my eyes were bugging right out of my head, I asked, "Ash. Wow. Who'd you kill?"

Behind me, River and Tarin laughed, and the large, bald guy with the tats leading us down the hall shot a raised eyebrow over his shoulder at us.

"Okay, I'm obviously missing something. Spill." I tugged Ash's hand, but he just kept pulling me along.

The empty hall didn't last long, eventually filling with workers from the club, doors here and there opening and closing. I'd never seen anything like it.

We finally came to a stop in front of one of the doors.

"Ya know what they're like before a gig, Ash," the big guy warned. "Ya on ya own from here."

As the guy walked away, Ash snorted and banged a fist on the door. "Y'all better put my sister's clothes back on!"

My legs went out from under me.

Thankfully, River caught me.

Sister? Did he say *sister*? What the...?

Ash flung open the door, and my brain tried to process what I saw. A black couch squatted on one side of the room, with a curly-haired blond sitting on it, his arms wrapped around the disheveled guy on his lap. Near a table filled with snacks, a girl with red hair was tugging a shirt over her head, while a third guy leaned against the wall, arms crossed over his chest, an amused smirk on his face.

I knew these people, even if I didn't know their names. This was Elemental Fallout. The two on the couch were the drummer and lead singer, and the other two were the guitarists.

Beside me, Ash threw his hands into the air. "Holy shit, you guys. I was joking!"

The guy against the wall grinned wider. "You know how they are when we perform." He shrugged, while amusement sparkled in his eyes. "Brooks and I find it's easier to just let them maul each other."

I glanced between the lead singer on the couch and the female guitarist. If they'd been making out, then why was the singer sitting in the drummer's lap?

Then, the drummer planted a kiss on the lead singer. "Company means playtime is over, babe."

Okay, was this a situation like what Maybell talked about? Were all of them dating each other? Or were only some of them dating? It was still a shock and exciting that dating more than one person in a Genus was not only accepted but the norm.

The confusion about the relationship dynamic helped me to suppress my urge to squeal. I was meeting rock stars! Real rock stars! Holy shit!

Tarin leaned close to whisper in my ear. "The blond is Brooks. The guy in his lap is Souta. Against the wall is JJ, and the redhead is Ash's little sister, Sera."

Ash's... Little... Sister. Holy shit. Brain. Fried.

Sera sauntered over to me, gave me an assessing look, and turned to her brother. "This is her?" At Ash's nod, she turned back to me. "Not what I expected. Are you sure she's a Quintus? I really thought they were a myth."

I wanted to be offended, but she didn't sound insulting. More confused, actually.

"It's the only thing that fits. We haven't figured

out her abilities yet, though." Ash hugged his sister, then ruffled her hair before coming to stand beside me.

Sera turned back to me. "Well, I can't imagine all of this is easy to adjust to when you didn't even know Elementum existed. These guys aren't easy to handle, so let me give you my number. When they start driving you bat shit, you can call me, and I'll give you all the dirty details on how to handle my brother's drama."

I couldn't help myself. I burst out laughing as I handed over my phone. "Got any advice for Zephyr?"

"Oh, the hot, grumpy asshole? Nope. Sorry. You're on your own with him," she said as she handed my phone back.

"Hey!" The growl from behind Sera drew my attention.

I didn't even notice Souta making his way in our direction.

He wrapped an arm around her waist and planted a kiss on her neck. "Aren't the three of us enough for you? No hot assholes allowed."

Sera spun, planted a kiss on Souta, then smacked his chest. "Shut it."

My curiosity from earlier returned. "Um, I have a

question I hope isn't rude."

Sera turned back to me.

"Are you all, um…" Hell, I didn't even know how to word my question. "Are you dating, like, um…"

Sera grinned. "I'm with all three of them, and Brooks and Souta are also together. I'm guessing my brother hasn't bothered mentioning it." She raised her brows, shooting Ash a look I couldn't read.

He shrugged.

"Don't be surprised, since he kept it a secret that you're his sister until two minutes ago," I told her with a look for Ash of my own.

He gave me an equally unapologetic look.

"Use my number," Sera advised me. "I can answer all the questions that my doofus brother doesn't."

The door cracked open, and a head poked around it. "Twenty minutes."

My phone chimed as the door closed.

Devin: Hey, we're here. Where are you?

Raegan: Be there in a second.

I glanced at Ash. "Hey, my brother and Pier are here."

"Okay, baby." He pressed a kiss to the top of my head. "We should let them get ready, anyway."

"I loved getting to meet you all," I gushed, unable

to hold in my enthusiasm. "I'm really looking forward to the show."

"You're gonna love it." Sera winked. "Seriously, use my number, 'kay?"

I nodded, still a bit overwhelmed.

My body hummed as we were led to the main club area.

Multicolored lights flashed and strobed overhead. People littered the small dance floor. At the far end of the club, a stage waited, instruments already set up. Tall tables waited at the edge of the dance floor, some with drinks but most abandoned.

We'd come out by the bar, which ran the length of this end of the club, the back wall mirrored with open shelving containing glasses and liquor.

I didn't anticipate the club being so crowded when I told Devin I'd find him. Or so dimly lit.

Turned out I didn't need to worry.

Ash grabbed my hand and navigated through the crowd, weaving among the tables closest to the dance floor. I spotted my brother and Pier before he did, sitting at one of the tall tables.

Of course, three girls already giggled and swooned by Devin while Pier hunched in his seat, looking for all the world like he wanted to disappear.

"Pier! Devin!" I hollered to be heard over the

music thumping through the speakers around the dance floor.

I tugged Ash's hand, directing him over to them.

River and Tarin stepped around us, grabbed a couple of abandoned chairs, and dragged them over to the table. Stopping next to Pier, I tried to pull my hand free from Ash, but apparently, he wasn't letting go.

Instead, I threw my free arm around Pier and hugged him tight.

I swore Ash growled, but I had to be hearing things, right?

"Hi! I'm so happy you're here!" I said excitedly. "You'll never believe what happened! I got to meet the band!"

One of the twits around Devin cackled. "Oh my God, you are so full of it. No one meets the band here."

Twit two snorted. "Right? Come on, how desperate do you have to be to make shit like that up?"

Twit three rolled her eyes. "Yeah, okay loser."

They turned back to Devin, giggles and flirts ready, only to freeze at the expression on his face.

Devin's eyes glittered with rage. "I think it's time you three leave."

The girls' jaws dropped, glares were sent in my direction, but after a minute or two of cold, hard Devin, they flounced off for better pickings.

"Finally," Pier sighed and rolled his eyes. "I'd love to go somewhere with you and not be accosted by bimbos."

Devin plopped his elbows on the table, rested his head in his hands, and batted his lashes. "Jealous?"

I cracked up. They were utterly ridiculous, the pair of them, and someday they'd both figure their shit out. I was going to enjoy the "I told you so" moment.

The thumping music cut off.

"I know why you're all here!" The DJ's voice echoed around the now quiet club.

At his words, a roar of excitement went up.

"Okay, okay. I know you're excited, but you can do better than that." He cupped his hand over his ear. "I don't think the band can hear you."

The whole club screamed and hollered again, the sound deafening.

My skin buzzed, and I bounced on the balls of my feet.

"Nope! Still not feeling it!" The DJ shook his head with exaggerated disappointment. "Who are we waiting for?"

"*Elemental Fallout!*" The entire club roared.

"One more time!"

"*Elemental Fallout!*"

I thought I might vibrate right out of my skin as the dark stage lit up, and Sera and her boys walked out.

Without a word, they launched into their first song, and the energy in the club burst right through the roof. The dance floor filled with people trying to get close to the stage, heads bopping and bodies shimmying to the music.

An arm settled on my shoulder.

With a glance, I confirmed the arm belonged to Ash.

On stage, the band rocked. Souta moved like sex incarnate, working the whole stage, moving between Sera and JJ, occasionally wandering back to Brooks on the drums. He flowed and shifted, everywhere at once.

Several songs in, a light stream of fire flew from Sera's fingertips on the downstroke.

I gasped. How could they get away with that?

Behind me, Ash leaned in close. "Watch, they've perfected this."

As the stream of flame headed for the stage, Souta slid across the stage, a glint of silver appearing in his hands. I couldn't tell from this distance what exactly it was, but Souta aimed it at the stream of fire, then flowed the whole thing over his head in a circle.

"Look close at Sera's fingers," Ash instructed.

When I looked, I noticed the tiniest of movements, and everything made sense. The silver wand thing was all for show, making it legit.

I paid closer attention after that and noticed they did several things in the same vein.

The time flew by, and the show was over before I even processed it.

As we made our way back to the car afterward, I knew I was in trouble. Every moment I spent with these three made that strange flutter inside grow stronger, and I was starting to suspect I knew what it was.

CHAPTER TWENTY

ASH

Normally, I enjoyed my evening walks, especially coming home from dinner at Dad's place, but with everything happening lately, I found myself on high alert. I didn't like being away from Rae, but at least, I knew she was safe tonight.

A few days had passed since we took her to the concert, and she'd been spending the evenings with Tarin and River, training more. My friends would keep her safe without me there.

Things were quiet lately. Too quiet. It bugged me and gave my mind time to wander and worry.

At dinner, Dad brought out an old photo album he'd found with pictures of him, my mom, Sera's mom, Tarin's mom, and River's stepdad. He thought

Sera might like to see the photos, see how close my mom and hers once were.

It brought Sera's sudden appearance into our lives blasting back into my mind. It'd been a year or so, but sometimes, it felt like I'd always had my sister.

I'd come a long way from the rage I'd felt when she first appeared on Dad's doorstep.

The problem was it brought back the memories of all the bad shit that happened to her around the same time. We could have lost her before we really found her. The asshole who'd been after her was dead, though. Sera had watched the car explode, barely escaping with her skin and life intact.

The guy couldn't still be around. It was impossible. Everything happening now with Rae, though, was eerily reminiscent of those times.

Could he have had followers? The way Sera and the guys described him, he'd just seemed like a nutball. Could he have convinced other Elementum he had valid ideas?

No. I was creating mountains out of nothing, inventing problems before they existed. I mean, yeah, someone wanted Rae, but with how quiet things had been since she moved in with us, maybe they'd given up and moved on to a new quarry.

After all, we still didn't know what Rae could do.

Not even May knew that. If whoever tried to kidnap Rae had been watching us, they'd likely figured out she didn't know her powers and went elsewhere.

Unless I had the whole thing wrong.

A horn honked, jolting me out of my thoughts.

Damn, I was in a mood tonight. Maybe the new moon made me forlorn or something. That was a thing that happened, right? Yeah, okay, even I didn't believe that.

My thoughts made my feet speed up. I needed to see Rae, to be sure she was okay even though I knew she'd been spending the evening with Tarin and River training some more.

After their fight, Zephyr refused to train with her.

I tucked my hands in my pockets as I walked. The cold metal of my lighter was a comfort as a shiver ran down my spine.

Eyes were on me. I could feel them.

I sped up more. Only a few blocks from home now.

Whoever watched me could keep watching, as long as that was all they did.

I didn't like it, though. There were few lights on this block, and a couple had burned out, creating dark pockets that didn't help my unease.

I gripped the lighter in my pocket tighter as I left the ring of light and stepped into darkness.

Arms came around me from behind, clamping down, and a deep, scratchy voice filled my ear. "Where's the girl?"

I wiggled and fought the arms encasing me, their steely strength making it difficult to move. They forgot about my feet, though, and I kicked their shin hard. My heel connected, followed by a grunt of pain.

The guy's arms tightened around me. "I'm not alone, you idiot. This can go very wrong for you."

As I pulled back my foot to strike another blow, wind swirled around them, forcing my legs together and holding them in place.

Okay, this asshole was pissing me off, but I couldn't let my tendency to blow a fuse take over right now. He hadn't moved his fingers to manipulate the wind around me, which meant he might be telling the truth. Few of us could control our element without directing it somehow.

"Go stick your dick in hot lava!" I shouted.

Drawing in a breath, I let myself go limp, so I didn't keep burning energy while I racked my brain. The air around me formed other bands around my legs, binding my arms so the asshole still holding me would have an easier time.

I needed to get this guy to let me go and somehow break the air bindings.

"I can make you wish you'd never met her. Make you hurt. Make you scream," the guy threatened. "But why should you suffer for an anomaly? A thing that shouldn't exist. Your Genus is completed. All she's doing is causing problems."

Oh, fuck no. My fists clenched within my pockets, and the hard corners of my lighter cut into my palm. I only needed a little movement of my fingers and…

Whoosh! Flame flared out of my pocket, followed by the smell of searing flesh seconds before the man's scream rang in my ears.

The arms released me, and I channeled my anger into the flames. Gathering them around me, I shoved the flames outward as hard as I could. It shouldn't work, but it did. The bands of wind around me broke.

Part of me wanted to stay and beat the crap out of these guys. The smarter part of my brain told me getting gone was a better idea.

After glancing at my black clad attacker— seriously did these guys all dress from the same closet? —I booked it while the asshole still screamed.

Thank the Elements for all the training I did,

because it meant I could sustain a good run all the way back to the house. I was also glad we didn't live too far from Dad.

Barreling through the front door, I threw the lock and pulled out my phone. The only good thing to come from the events last year with my sister was that I had two members of the Lex on speed dial.

I hit a number as I stormed into the kitchen.

"Quin," said a voice in greeting when the phone picked up.

"It's Sera's brother, Ash." I knew he'd remember Sera. Quin was not only a Lex, but a Seer, an incredibly rare gift, and he'd had a horrible vision of Sera. "I need to report an attack."

I rattled off my address since he'd only ever been to Dad's before, and he promised to be right over.

"Attack?" River's bark made me jump.

With frantic motions, I waved at him to quiet down. The last thing I wanted was to worry Rae.

"Rae isn't here. She went to her folk's house for dinner or something." River pulled me into the kitchen and shoved me toward the dining table. "Now, what's this about being attacked?"

Adrenaline finally wearing off, I sank into a chair. "On my way back tonight, a guy jumped out of nowhere. Of course, I was lost in my head. Didn't even notice him."

"Notice who?" Zephyr asked as he sauntered in. "Where's the interloper?"

His eyes did a quick scan, and something flashed in them too quickly for me to catch.

Was he finally feeling something other than annoyance toward our girl?

"Not here," River snapped. "Now, sit while Ash tells us about his attackers."

"Attackers?" Zephyr dropped to a chair, and Tarin joined us from wherever he'd been hiding in the house.

That made everyone. Great, I wouldn't have to repeat myself a million times.

"Anyway," I continued. "On the way home, this guy comes out of nowhere, gets the drop on me, and wants to know 'where the girl is', which I assumed meant Rae."

"Fudge," Tarin cursed. "I was kind of hoping they'd given up."

Hearing my earlier thoughts echoed helped with the guilt I'd been feeling.

"What the hell do we do now?" Tarin demanded.

"We watch our backs, protect our girl, and bring

in the big guns," I said as a knock sounded on the door.

Standing, I walked back to the entry and opened it to find Quin standing on the other side. His partner, Braxton, hovered protectively behind him.

"Hey, thanks for coming." I stepped back to let them inside. "Didn't know it required both of you to make a report."

Quin blushed as his gaze darted to his partner. "Since we aren't on shift, it normally wouldn't, but I don't go anywhere without my...anchor."

That was new. So was the hand Braxton placed on Quin's back, just above his ass. Made me wonder what happened with them in the last year.

I had other priorities, though.

Braxton and Quin followed me into the kitchen, where the others still waited.

As we sat at the table, Tarin set a carafe--which I didn't know we'd owned--on the table along with two mugs joining the other mugs and the sugar and creamer already there.

Quin reached for a mug and filled it, taking a deep sniff before relaxing back and taking a sip of the hot coffee. "Okay, fill us in."

I went into a bit more detail for them than I did with the guys, noting that I hadn't actually seen another person, so I couldn't verify more than one attacker.

When I told them I got a good look at him, Braxton pulled out a small recorder and asked to describe him in as much detail as possible.

Thankfully, I'd spent enough time around Sera's artist boyfriend to know what details they were looking for. I didn't know how much they'd be able to do about the attack, but if they had a picture, a visual, maybe it would help.

As I finished, a thought occurred to me.

I turned to River. "How long until our girl comes home?"

He shrugged. "I can text Devin and have him make sure she doesn't come back for a bit."

Okay, this could work.

"Yeah, okay." I swiveled my gaze to Quin. "Can you see current stuff or just the future?"

Quin's eyes widened. "I don't know. I've never tried to actively seek a vision. Is that something Seers can do?"

I blinked, my brain stuttering at his words. "Didn't you get taught this stuff when you were training your powers?"

"I didn't know what I was," he said defensively. "I'm still figuring it out."

A million more questions filled my mind, but they could wait. This was more important.

"Seers were born from Ignis," I explained, "from a secondary ability that let us look into flames and see things, far away, current, past, future. It varied for each Ignis with the ability. Even though you're rare, there's some documentation of Seers being able to do the same, not just see the future."

Braxton's arm snaked around Quin's waist, and he pulled him against his side. "I'm right here, Quin. Always. It's your choice."

Again, so many questions, but not the time. I wanted information, and I hoped Quin could help us get it because I was so done with our girl being in danger.

Quin bit his lip, gaze unfocusing for a second before returning to me. He shuddered and squared his shoulders. "Is it just because of this attack, to get revenge on this guy?"

I knew why he asked that. I didn't know much about him, but he always struck me as upstanding, so he wouldn't help me if I was in it for my own purposes. "No. This guy was interested in Rae. I don't think he's the one behind the attempts on her previously, though. I don't care about this guy. Hopefully, you can see the one behind those attacks and help us be proactive. I'm sick of them coming out of nowhere. If we had a little information, we could protect her better."

For a moment, I thought Quin would refuse, but then he nodded. "Okay. I understand that, but I can't make promises. I've never sought out a regular vision, and I still need fire."

Grinning, I flicked my lighter. "Fire we have."

He laughed.

Standing, I motioned for them to follow me, and I led the way to the living room, which had a fireplace. "I'm sure this will work better than my lighter, though."

"Infinitely." Quin sank down in front of the fireplace as Tarin got a fire going.

Braxton sat beside him, a hand at the small of his back. No one spoke as we all settled around the room, giving Quin and Brax a bit of space.

For a while, the fire blazed and crackled, the only sound beyond breathing to be heard while we waited, the tension so thick in the air it could have been cut with a knife.

Then, Quin began to speak.

CHAPTER TWENTY-ONE

TARIN

A man stands in a room, brown hair falling at an angle over his face and obscuring one eye. A frown pulls down the corners of his mouth, and he wrinkles his forehead as he stares at the woman facing him, one hand on her hip. Only a couple inches shorter, she comes close to meeting his eyes. Neither is remarkable in any way in appearance, especially the man.

In a crowd, a person would overlook him.

"What about the room?" Ash asked.

The room holds a large bed with a garish floral comforter. Two dark wood nightstands sit on either side, and a matching double dresser squats opposite the end of the bed. A television rests on the top. At the far end, a long counter holds a sink with a mirror over it, drawers *and cabinets beneath. A door is closed to one side, presumably hiding the bathroom. A round table and two chairs sit at the other end of the room, to the right of the door and in front of a large window.*

"Great. Sounds like every motel room on every corner," I grumbled. "That's not much help."

The pair are arguing.

"What are they saying? Can you hear them?" Sitting on the couch, I rest my arms on my knees.

"How can you keep messing this up?" The woman leans forward, getting in the man's face.

"I'm not messing up. They are," the man protests.

"You have no control over them, Joshua," she sneers. "You send them out unprepared. How are you ever going to get what we need that way?"

Joshua backs up and turns away. He runs a hand through his hair, messing up the careful styling. "We will get the girl." It's a snarl of words. "We have to. There's no other choice."

"Do you even know why we need her?" she demands. "Why is she so important?"

Joshua whirls, his face contorted in anger. "The Enlightened one says we need her. That is all we need to know. I will bring her in myself if need be. No more idiots who can't grab a single girl."

The woman shakes her head, then leaves without another word.

"Dissent in the ranks? That can't be good." River spoke up. "We have a name for the guy, at least. Did you pick up anything about the woman?"

Quin shook his head. "Blond hair, average—Wait. Something's happening. Oh shit, guys…"

Joshua paces to the nightstand and picks up something resting on the top. A photo.

Staring up at him, a woman smiles. A woman with pale hair, nearly white, straight, and hanging past her shoulders. Soft features, pale skin, blue eyes. Joshua stands next to her, an arm over her shoulders, a wide grin on his face. Behind them, three other men grin at the camera. None of them touch the woman, but their eyes rest on her. They're interested, attracted, but the body language speaks to caution, to holding themselves back.

"I don't think the three in the back are involved with the girl," Quin adds. "But it's obvious they wanted to… Wait…"

Joshua runs a finger over the woman's face, his own features softening, his eyes unfocusing. "Soon, my love. My beautiful Alyssa. Soon, you'll be back where you belong. With me. And the Enlightened one promised we'd be able to restore you. We'll bring you back to yourself."

Quin shook himself and turned from the fire. "I can't convey it any other way, but the girl in the photo… This Alyssa?" He scanned the room, meeting the gazes of all four men seated around him. "She's your Raegan."

"That's bullshit," Zephyr spoke from where he leaned against the wall by the entry. "No way is our Raegan this Alyssa."

"No, I don't mean literally." Quin sank against Braxton, weariness etched into every line of his face. "I mean, they could be twins. I don't know Joshua's mind, but I think he believes that it's literal."

"That's not good." Zephyr frowned.

"Anything else you remember? I won't ask you to look again. You're obviously exhausted," Ash said.

Quin shook his head, leaning more heavily on Braxton.

Braxton kissed the top of his head. "Thank you for not asking more."

"I wish I could have seen something more concrete for you." Quin's gaze drifted aimlessly as he and Braxton stood. They landed on the fire again, and he suddenly stiffened.

Joshua stares down at the photo, his finger running over the woman again. A frown crosses his face as he glances at the others, then it twists into a snarl.

He crumples the photo in a fist, then throws it to the floor. "This time no other shall covet what belongs to me. I'll eliminate anyone who dares."

With his last words, Quin collapsed.

Braxton cursed and caught him, folding him into a bridal-style carry. "Dammit. Pushed too far. What the fuck am I for if I can't prevent him from doing this?"

I stepped forward and placed a hand on Braxton's arm. "I don't know much about how any of this works, but I don't think there was anything you could have done to prevent that. Don't beat yourself up."

Braxton nodded, then carried his unconscious partner out.

I turned to the others. "It sounds like this guy is coming after us next. We better be prepared."

Zephyr pushed off the wall. "The interloper is trouble. I told you all nothing good could come of this. We should have let her be."

He turned to leave, only to find himself face-to-face with the very girl he'd been speaking of.

CHAPTER TWENTY-TWO

RAEGAN

*Z*ephyr shoved past me as my mind spun. What had I walked in on? Why were the Lex who'd taken my statement after that man broke into my house and tried to kidnap me here now?

The guilty looks that crossed the guys' faces didn't bode well for not upsetting me.

After only a couple of steps, Zephyr's footsteps stopped retreating.

I ignored that oddity in favor of the bigger one in front of me. "What's going on?"

"Hey, baby." Ash sidled up to me and wrapped an arm around my waist. Tingles raced down my spine at his touch. "Nothing to worry about. The Lex just wanted to keep us updated on the case. Not much movement, unfortunately."

"So, why is one passed out?" I demanded.

Ash's gaze slid away from me. "Uh, he hasn't been sleeping well. That's all."

I tilted my head, smiled at him, and batted my eyelashes. "Hey, Ash?"

Ash's shoulders relaxed, and he squeezed me as he waited for me to continue.

"Do you know what my grades were in school?" Sweetness dripped from my words like melting chocolate.

Ash shook his head.

"I was an honor roll student," I informed him. "That means I don't miss much, you know?"

"Uh…" Ash's arm fell from my waist, and he stepped back as he eyed me warily. "Okay?"

My tone went from sweet to steel. "So, why would you think I'd buy that bag of lies?"

They were going to tell me what was happening because it obviously involved me. I might not understand how to access my power, but I'd be damned if they started hiding shit from me.

Tarin sighed. "We didn't want you to worry. Ash was…confronted on his way home."

It sounded more like a question at the end.

"Confronted?" I turned my attention back to Ash.

Ash's shoulders slumped in defeat. "On my way home, this guy grabbed me from behind and asked me where the girl was. He's obviously connected to your attempted kidnapping, so I called the Lex. Quin is a Seer who uses fire, and when he glanced into ours, he accidentally got overwhelmed and passed out."

I felt like there might be more to it than that, but I wouldn't push. They'd told me most of it, and honestly, I didn't think I wanted to know what the Seer glimpsed in our fire.

"We should get going." Braxton cradled Quin closer and headed for the door, which meant I needed to move.

When I stepped out of the way, Zephyr still stood in the foyer, listening to everything.

I met his gaze with my own, daring him without words.

He scowled before turning and stomping up the stairs. I was over this, so very over it.

Leaving the guys to see the Lex out, I followed Zephyr up the stairs and to his room. Whatever his problems with me, we were going to resolve things tonight.

Apparently, Zephyr had some inkling of my state of mind because his bedroom door, normally closed, stood open. He laid out on his bed, shirt off—which, *yum*, thank you—and hands behind his head.

When I entered, he shot a scowl in my direction.

"We can't keep doing this," I said as I sank onto the end of his bed.

I'd never been in his room before and took a moment to look around. His bed dominated the space with a soft, airy blue comforter. A light wood nightstand, dresser, and desk took up the remaining space. The thing I noticed most, though, was the complete lack of decoration. No posters or pictures on the wall. No photo frames on the dresser. His desk was pin neat, not a thing out of place.

Actually, that was true of the whole room. I knew he was a bit of a neat freak, but that couldn't have anything to do with this lack of decoration, or framed photos, could it? Where were the pictures of the important people in his life, parents, best friends, siblings? I wanted to ask, but it wasn't the time to get into that. Right now, we needed to work out the issues between us.

Zephyr still hadn't said anything, so I turned my attention back to him. "Come on. You can't hate me this much."

Zephyr rolled his eyes and blew out a sigh. "I don't hate you."

All I could do was stare, hard. He'd been actively against me from the start.

"Look, I'm not going to bare my soul to you or anything. Let's just say, I don't trust easily. I don't let people in. I have my reasons. And this whole situation"—he waved a hand as if encompassing the whole room and leaned forward—"there's something off about it. There are too many questions and not enough answers. You're supposed to be something special in our world, something unique and rare, but despite all the training we've been doing with you, there's not a spark of power at all. Just nothing. And no one can tell us what there's supposed to be. That doesn't set off alarm bells to you?"

I hadn't considered things that way before. "Honestly, I've been so busy trying to wrap my head around the reality of the Elementum that I never thought of that. I assumed I was blocking myself. But that doesn't explain everything, Z."

"I know it doesn't. I'm just…" He threw his hands up. "I don't know. Everything has been chaos since you came around. Ash and Tarin are best friends, did you know that? Best friends since they were in diapers. I've never seen them so much as irritated with each other. Yet, they've been arguing since you got here. And River is busy all the time with work, but he used to spend his spare with me. I've barely seen him lately because he wants to be in your orbit."

That second part made me stop and wonder. "Z. Are you…jealous? Is there something—"

"*What?*" He jerked back. "No!"

I wasn't buying it. There may or may not be something between them. It didn't matter to me, but he was for sure jealous.

"It's nothing like that. You just…" He blew out a breath, the fight going out of him as he collapsed against the headboard. "These guys are all I have. They're my *family*. And ever since you showed up in our lives, they've been in danger, and not just from outside forces. If you're here, do we even stand a chance of continuing as a Genus?"

He wouldn't meet my eyes and honestly, I didn't think I could handle it if he did. I knew nothing about him or his past. I had a feeling, though, that he didn't talk like this often, if ever. He didn't make himself vulnerable, but he had. For me. I respected that.

"That's not my fault, you know," I pointed out.

"I've not exactly had an easy time, and you've done nothing to help."

Damn. Now, I felt like I was attacking him. My words weren't coming out right, and my head couldn't get straight. Too many feelings going on for me to nail one down.

For a moment, anger flared out of nowhere. I shoved it out, as it was unproductive.

Zephyr's face twisted in a scowl, angrier than I'd ever seen.

What the hell?

Zephyr shuddered, and the scowl cleared from his face, confusion following it. "Did you feel that?"

Unsure of what he meant, I shook my head.

"You didn't feel it? The spike of pure fury that just got speared into my brain?"

What the...? I didn't know where the anger I'd felt came from, but I knew I'd pushed it away. And then, he'd felt it?

"I felt a spike of anger just before you did. I, uh, pushed it away, but..." I didn't know what else to say, but Zephyr didn't seem to need my words.

Of course, that didn't mean he used his own words.

We sat there in silence for a minute.

"Try it again." Zephyr sat forward and grabbed

my hand. "A different emotion this time. Make yourself feel it, really feel it, then push it out."

I shook my head. "Why?"

"I have an idea," he said. "Something Ash mentioned once."

Sure. Why not?

"Okay." I hesitated, uncertain where to start.

Anger was a strong emotion. Would I need one as strong as that? I sifted through my memories, trying to find one that invoked such a strong emotion. I had a lot of wonderful memories, lots of joy and love, but I needed an emotion that would be out of place.

Then, my mind drifted back to the year I turned eight. The fevers, the seizures, the hospitals, the total lack of answers, the looks on the faces of my parents, my brother, the doctors. I'd never been more terrified —not before and not since—for my very life.

I let that feeling fill me, take over, then shoved it toward Zephyr.

Eyes going wide, he doubled over, his limbs shaking.

It took him a minute or two longer to shake off the feeling this time, but when he finally did, he looked up at me. "Holy shit. What was that? When the hell would you ever have had the chance to be that terrified?"

Not ready to share that with him, I shook my head. It wasn't something I wanted to relive, and using it for this had been hard enough.

"Yeah, okay. I get it. Off-limits," he said without me having to explain. "But I'm pretty sure I have my answer. You have some kind of empathic ability. At the very least, you can make me feel what you're feeling."

"But…No…What…" Worry clouded my mind. I didn't want to mess up other peoples' emotions. That wasn't right. Besides…I looked at Z. "What the heck am I supposed to do with that? I don't want to force emotions onto people."

Zephyr shook his head. "I don't know, but it's something, at least." He paused, and I could almost see his mind working, his feelings twisting, and finally his resignation. "You're right, you know. You didn't ask for any of this. You're going through a bunch of shit of your own. Shit I'm familiar with. And I'm making it worse." He met my eyes, his gaze still wary but the hard, steel cold was gone. "Look, I don't trust you, and I don't trust the situation. To be honest, I don't trust, well, much of anything. But I can stop being an asshole."

My smile about broke my face. "Thank you. I'll prove to you I'm worth your trust. I swear."

Zephyr snorted. "Don't make promises you can't keep, troublemaker."

Knowing that was as good as I would get, I turned without another word, letting him have his win. The best rewards, the ones that meant the most, were the ones fought hardest for, and I had a feeling Zephyr would give me a run for my money.

In the end, though, I would earn his friendship, and when I did, it would be the sweetest reward I'd ever gained.

CHAPTER TWENTY-THREE

RAEGAN

The last couple days had been pleasant without the animosity from Zephyr.

He wasn't warm and welcoming, but I didn't expect him to be. He'd told me he wouldn't be after all. Still, no snarky, nasty remarks or hate-filled glares meant a pleasant few days.

The boys came and went, but they were reluctant for me to go anywhere on my own. That didn't mean I was stuck in the house; it just meant I didn't get out a lot. They seemed shocked and a little wary of my power, but honestly, they could join the club. I hated the idea of being able to project my emotions at people. I'd spent a good portion of the last few days trying to figure out this empathic ability with little success.

After another fruitless attempt to feel any smidgen of power in my body, I threw myself onto my bed as my phone chimed. A glance at the screen revealed someone who could most definitely help take my mind off my issue.

I answered. "Hey Pier. What's up?"

"Not much. How are things in the house of hot men?" he asked, sounding distracted.

I frowned. "What's wrong?"

"Nothing." His voice rose at the end, false happiness lacing every syllable. "I'm just calling my BFF to catch up."

Glaring at the phone, I put on my sternest voice. "Don't bullshit me."

Pier sighed. "Okay, look, I really need to talk to you. Think you can drag yourself away from your eye candy for a bit?"

With everything happening lately, even Pier and Devin had been extra careful when I went out. Neither of them ever asked for me on my own. This had to be major for Pier to ask me to come without a babysitter, and I had a feeling I knew what it was about.

I wouldn't betray him by bringing anyone with me. "Yeah, it's not a big deal. Where do you want to meet?"

"What about that little park near you?" he offered. "The spot where the coffee cart usually parks? Isn't there an area that's a bit, um, private?"

I knew which park he referred to, and it wasn't too far away. I could walk without issue, and near the coffee cart was an area with benches, surrounded by several flower beds and a couple young trees on three sides. It wasn't totally secluded or tucked away or anything like that, but it offered a semblance of privacy.

"Yeah, I know where you mean. Fifteen minutes?" That should give him enough time to get there.

Relief and worry filled his voice. "Yeah, see you in a few."

We hung up, and I strode to my dresser. Since I spent so much time at the house right now, I'd taken to wearing tiny sleep shorts and a tank top. Deciding to leave the tank on, I slipped on a pair of jeans, tossed a hoodie over the tank, and grabbed my sneakers.

I sat on the top step to put them on before dashing down the stairs and hollering out, "Going for a walk. Back in a few."

Without giving them a chance to stop me, I dashed out the door. They wouldn't want to let me go on my own, and Pier wouldn't be able to say what he needed to with them hovering around.

It didn't take long to find my way to the meeting spot. Dark clouds rolled slowly across the sky, and wind blew through me, straight to my bones.

I grabbed a couple coffees from the cart to keep us warm. There was a line at the coffee cart, but not many people in the park. That made my stomach clench. Maybe we should have met somewhere more crowded. And perhaps indoors.

I glanced at my phone.

No texts from Pier, so he was still heading my way.

Maybe I should suggest a change of venue for this talk? Although, I didn't think Pier would prefer a crowded place where people could overhear.

A sharp whistle split the air, followed by Pierson's voice, "Rae!"

I turned toward the shout and spotted him strolling toward me from across the park, one hand tucked in his jeans pocket, the other fidgeting at his side.

"Hey, I got your fav." I held up the coffee cup, then indicated the dark clouds. "Should we find cover?"

Pier shook his head. "Aren't there pavilions and such around the lake?"

I nodded. It was more of a pond, actually, but the park had a couple of pavilions, not to mention a few buildings, maintenance, restrooms, and other places with overhangs. If we got caught in a downpour, we could find cover. I hadn't heard any thunder yet, so I thought we'd likely be okay.

He took his coffee from me, then nodded toward the pond. "Let's walk. I'm not sure I can sit right now."

"Everything okay?" I asked more to fill the quiet that descended as our feet found the path.

When Pier said nothing, I let it be. This was his moment, and whatever he wanted, whether or not it was what I suspected, needed to happen in his own time and his own way. No matter how hard I wanted to hug him right now.

Figuring this was a good time to practice my new empathy abilities, I tried to fill myself with feelings of calm and confidence.

The first time I'd done it, with Zephyr, I'd needed to use a memory to help me feel the right emotion.

Since then, I'd been purposefully bringing different memories to mind in the evenings and memorizing the way they made me feel, trying to get myself used to them so they'd be automatic when I needed them.

Most were still pretty elusive without a memory, especially the strongest ones, but calm and confidence I'd manage to do.

With those filling me, I gave a gentle shove in Pierson's direction. This part I hadn't practiced yet, so it was rougher than I'd wanted.

Pier shivered, then his face relaxed. "I've been struggling lately. A lot. Did you ever have a time when you thought you knew who you were, really and truly knew, but then something happened that sent your whole sense of self spinning out of control?"

Our walk stalled as Pier turned to face me.

"No. I don't think I've ever really felt like I truly knew exactly who I was. Maybe because there's so much mystery around my birth and my birth parents and such. I mean, Devin was too little to remember his parents when they died, but our parents were able to tell him a few things when he asked. Mine..." I shrugged because there wasn't much else to do.

Even the great Sage, Maybell, didn't know who my birth parents were, who'd given me to my folks, or what happened to him. I had texted her after our first meeting as questions popped up, but she didn't know any more than my adopted parents did.

I gave Pier another push of confidence as I add, "But I know what it feels like to have your world turned upside down."

Oh yeah, that was a feeling I still struggled with.

Pier nodded, then continued walking, his fingers going back to fidgeting at his side. "Well, that happened to me when you moved to town."

I blinked a few times at that, unsure what he meant.

"I mean, here you were, so beautiful and sweet and amazing in so many ways." He flapped a hand up and down at me. "And for some reason, out of everyone at school, you chose me to latch on to. And then it was like we just…fit, you know?"

Oh, shit. No. Please tell me I hadn't gotten this so entirely wrong. I didn't have those kinds of feelings for him.

"I dated plenty before you came here," he continued. "I have my share of exes, but no one ever came close to you. Here you were, this amazing girl that was absolutely perfect for me in every way, who I rarely fought with, who just completed me."

Oh fuck, oh fuck, oh fuck. How did you stop someone from telling you they loved you and not totally destroy them? Oh my God. I had to do something. This could not happen.

"But…" He paused to gather himself.

I liked *but*. Keep going with *but*. That was my new favorite word. *But.*

"All I could think about was tattoos and piercings and combat boots and someone who was so far from everything I supposedly knew I wanted." He stopped to look around, then headed to a nearby bench and sat.

A relieved breath escaped me as I joined him.

"And that person was a guy." He searched my face for a reaction, so I smiled, reached out for his hand, and squeezed.

I didn't want to say anything yet, not when it felt like there was more. I hadn't known he was struggling with his attraction to Devin, that it was new for him. It seemed that he needed to talk to work a few things out still. I could reassure him I was okay with it without words for now.

"I'd never dated a guy before, and this…this crush came out of left field. My exes are all girls. The more I thought it over, though, I realized I'd had hints for a while. I don't suppose too many guys notice how another guy looks." He snorted and ran a hand through his hair. "I kept trying to ignore it, you know? I figured it would go away as so many other crushes had, but for whatever reason, it keeps sticking around." Pier slumped. "I'm tired of fighting it."

"Pier, I hope you know you're my best friend, and I love you no matter what." I needed him to know I would still be here for him. "But can we talk about this crush on my brother now?" I grinned, trying to lighten the moment.

"Ugh!" Pier threw up his hands and spun on the bench to face me. "Why? Why did I have to choose him for my bi-awakening? The guy who's got every damn girl around throwing themselves at him?"

I laughed and tried to decide if I wanted to reassure him or not. Oh hell, I couldn't let him stew. "I'm pretty sure Devin likes you, too."

Pier sat up straight so fast I feared he might break something.

I grinned. "You should go for it."

His cheeks flushed, and a panicked look entered his eyes. "Okay, okay, let's talk about something else before my poor little heart bursts from too much hope."

A loud crack of thunder tore through the sky, followed by a streak of bright lightning.

Fuck. We should probably find cover.

"Let's head to that little bakery a block or so away." I glanced up at the sky, just noticing how much darker it got. "Before we become drowned rats."

Pier nodded, and we headed off at a fast clip, neither of us talking while we concentrated on power walking out of the park.

Movement caught my eye. A glance revealed a flash of red shirt and brown hair. I frowned as I spun toward the sight, peering closer. Something about it knocked on my brain.

When a fat drop of rain landed on my face, I put it from my mind as Pier and I dashed for one of the pavilions nearby.

CHAPTER TWENTY-FOUR

ZEPHYR

Go for a walk? Was the girl crazy? Did she forget that someone kept trying to kidnap her? Fucking idiot. She shouldn't be out by herself.

Throwing on my sneakers, I didn't let myself think about what I was doing. The girl might be annoying and causing issues, but she was ours, dammit. We'd keep her safe.

"I'm following Rae!" I hollered as I headed for the stairs.

Ash poked his head out of his door. He'd been locked in his room all day, not letting any of us in. At least, he wasn't hanging all over the girl and fighting with Tarin. "Did you just use her name?"

I scowled at him.

He held up his hands. "Okay, okay. I won't mention it. Right now. No promises for later, though. Go follow our girl. She shouldn't be out alone."

As he ducked back inside, I called out, "What the hell are you doing in there, anyway?"

He didn't respond, likely not hearing me, and I didn't have time to follow up with him if I wanted to catch our girl.

Thankfully, she hadn't gotten too far ahead of me. Just far enough to not notice me.

My eyes narrowed on her purposeful stride. She didn't look like a girl just out for a stroll. Where was she going?

Our walk took us to a nearby park. Was she wanting a stroll around the pond here?

Actually, why the hell did she suddenly decide to go for a walk? And why the heck did she keep walking when the clouds looked so ominous? Normally, that would deter people from an outing. What was she up to? I didn't think she had nefarious purposes. I'd never truly thought that. But I didn't like when things didn't add up, and nothing about her added up.

A coffee truck sat near the park. Browns, creams, and blacks splashed over the sides in an artist's rendering of spilled coffee. Coffee beans and cups decorated the sides as well.

Raegan got in the line at the truck. Lingering on the fringes of the park so I wouldn't be noticed, I waited for a few more customers to fill in the space behind her. I didn't drink coffee, but I loved a good chai or even a good hot chocolate.

When Rae was about halfway to the truck, I joined the line.

I kind of wished I grabbed a hat, but it didn't appear our girl was even remotely suspicious. It annoyed me that she wasn't paying more attention to her surroundings. Someone tried to kidnap her, for Element's sake!

Wait, why did she have two cups of coffee? Was she meeting her brother? Or maybe…

A whistle caught my attention, followed by the sound of Rae's name being shouted.

Sure enough, that friend of Raegan's, Pierson, strolled up to her, took the second cup of coffee, and they headed toward the pond.

I didn't trust that guy. Okay, I didn't trust anyone who I didn't consider family, but I *really* didn't trust that guy. Weird shit kept happening when he was around. Having an inside person, someone close to the mark, would certainly make things easier for the people trying to kidnap Raegan.

"Hey, order or move, please." The biting words yanked my attention back to the cart, and the annoyed face of the barista who waited on me.

"Uh, sorry. Got distracted." I glanced back toward Rae to see they weren't moving fast. "Large chai, please."

The girl nodded, took my payment, and I stepped to the side to wait for my drink.

Another check on Raegan and her friend gave me doubts about my original assessment. His body language didn't look like a guy trying to get a mark alone. His face was drawn tight, shoulders hunched. He was like a peanut, curling up on himself.

Once I had my drink in hand—and holy cow, that was good—I made my way close enough to hear. Thankfully, the path around the lake was surrounded by several trees and flower beds, so staying out of sight was easier than I thought it would be. As they walked, neither of them bothered to look around.

When I got Raegan home, she was getting the reaming out of her life.

The blond guy's words caught my attention. "Did you ever have a time when you thought you knew who you were, really and truly knew, but then something happened that sent your whole sense of self spinning out of control?"

I knew that feeling. Knew it all too well. And I was right. This guy needed his best friend. Didn't mean he was trustworthy, but at least, I knew this time his reasons were genuine.

Listening to Raegan's reply struck home with me, too. I could understand her feeling so well. I'd never felt like I knew who I was, either. Not until I found the guys.

Dammit. I didn't want to feel any kind of connection or sympathy for Raegan. How could I not, though? She'd told me before that she was struggling, but I'd ignored it, too caught up in my anger and suspicion. But now, I realized how lost she must feel, thrown into this world of ours, the same way I'd been when River found me.

"Well, that happened to me when you moved to town. I mean, here you were, so beautiful and sweet and amazing in so many ways. And for some reason, out of everyone at school, you chose me to latch on to. And then, it was like we just…fit, you know?"

Oh, for fuck's sake. Was this guy about to tell our Raegan he was in love with her? What the hell was it about this girl that had everyone falling over themselves?

The sky darkened overhead, the storm clouds rolling in faster, and I glanced around. For the most part, people were heading swiftly toward the parking lot, trying to beat the oncoming rain. A few seemed determined to wait it out by the lake, or maybe they were stupidly hopeful.

A flash of red caught my eye, ducking behind a tree a little too close to Rae and her friend for my comfort.

Slowing my steps, I let a bit more space fall between me and them, keeping an eye on the spot I'd seen the red shirt. Another flash of red. Another tree, a little too close.

Someone was definitely following our girl.

"I'd never dated a guy before and this…this crush came out of left field."

Huh, so not our girl, then. Good. Peanut could keep his grubby mitts away from our Raegan.

Movement drew my eye. Mr. Red Shirt wasn't even trying for stealthy, anymore. He openly stalked.

Nope. Not this time. Rae was our girl, and no one was taking her from us. Not now. Not ever. I didn't care what these freaks wanted.

I lengthened my pace to catch up with Rae. I needed to get her out of here. Now.

Neither of them turned at the sound of my swift steps behind them.

Fucking idiots. Seriously? I was definitely giving Rae a piece of my mind. A part of me wanted to scare her, to grab her from her behind and make her wake the fuck up about the danger she'd put herself in.

Except she was actually in danger right now, so probably not the time.

I stepped even with them and growled under my breath, "You're a fucking moron."

They both started, and color crept over Raegan's cheeks.

"You're being fucking stalked right now, and there aren't a whole lot of people around," I continued. "What the fuck were you thinking going out by yourself?"

"I asked her to come." Peanut rounded on me, shoulders squared and a fierce glare on his face. The effect he wanted was ruined, though, by the fat drops of rain falling lazily and plastering his hair to his head. "I needed my best friend without all of you overprotective asses around."

I wanted to argue with him, but we didn't have time for that.

"We'll finish this later. We need to go." I wrapped

a hand around Raegan's arm and dragged her toward the end of the park where we'd come in.

"I thought we agreed to try getting along, but now, you're being as much of an ass as ever. What the fuck?" After a handful of steps, she yanked out of my grasp and backed away.

It took a minute for me to react, to stop the forward motion of my feet. Same for her friend.

That minute, that small space, was all he needed.

Red Shirt grabbed her before I could say anything.

Raegan shouted, but not loud enough for anyone to hear her. Most people had vacated by now.

Fuckity fuck. This guy wasn't getting our girl. I tried to follow but ran into an invisible wall. A quick glance revealed Peanut running into the same issue.

Fuck! What the hell was going on?

Red Shirt dragged her, but our girl dug her heels into the wet grass.

Good girl.

My heart pounded when Red Shirt lifted her enough to no longer be touching the ground and strode away faster than it seemed like any person should be able to.

I gathered a bit of the air into a tight ball, prayed

it would go through whatever barrier was blocking us, and tossed it.

Red Shirt didn't flinch or slow down. Did it even impact? What the fuck was going on here?

Next to me, Peanut thrust a hand out. "Stop!"

What the fuck did he think that...would...do? Was that an arrow of rain?

My gaze darted to Peanut.

Did he throw that out?

No, now wasn't the time. We needed to get Raegan away from her abductor.

Turning back, I cursed to see how much distance Red Shirt had put between us.

Fuck. Our girl didn't have any way to stop him. Empathy wouldn't help her here.

I gathered more air into a ball and lobbed it, one after the other.

Peanut tried shaking his hand, but no more arrows of water appeared. "I don't know what the fuck I just did!"

Without looking away or breaking my tosses, I yelled, "Well, whatever it was, fucking do it again!"

From the corner of my eye, I saw him copying my movements, and suddenly, balls of rain followed my balls of air.

But everything we threw at the kidnapper bounced right off.

What the fuck was up with this guy? Frustration poured through me, and I pounded against the barrier, except the barrier wasn't there anymore, and I stumbled forward.

After I regained my feet, I shot a look to Peanut, who was now free, too. We dashed after Red Shirt and Rae as they neared the road. We weren't going to make it. There was still too much distance between us.

I sent a stream of air to trip him.

As if he saw the attack, he jumped, releasing Rae for a second when he stumbled. Before I could even shout at Rae to run or she could do it herself, Red Shirt recovered and snatched her up again, continuing the run to the road.

By all the Elements! What the hell was up with this guy?

One of Peanut's water balls smacked him just as a car careened to a stop right beside him.

No. No. No. No.

I threw out another rope of air, and a similar one of water flowed along the same path, the stream a bit disorganized.

Red Shirt threw open the back door and jumped

in, yanking a screaming Rae with him. Water splashed her ankles, which meant my air did as well, moments before the door slammed closed.

I tried to get a visual on the driver and failed miserably.

As the car took off, I used every curse I knew and made up a few more.

A hand clamped down on my shoulder. "I got the plate. I'll call the cops."

The words calmed my brain, and I grabbed Peanut's wrist as he raised his phone.

"No. they can't help. Go back to the house and get the others. They'll know the proper authority to call. I'm following that car." I released his wrist and raced for the parking lot.

"You'll never catch them on foot!" he hollered after me.

"Not planning to go on foot!" I hollered back. "And we'll talk about what you did when we get our girl back!"

I didn't bother waiting to see if Peanut did what I told him to. I had to trust he wanted to help Raegan as much as I did. I made it to the lot and looked around for a good mark. I didn't have the most law-abiding childhood. Thankfully, I'd not gotten caught before I went straight, and those skills were like riding a bike.

Finally, I found what I was looking for at the back of the lot. An old car, a good twenty-five, maybe thirty years old, made before a lot of the anti-theft things came standard.

I ran for it.

"Hey!" someone shouted from behind me.

Fuck.

I stopped, then turned, praying whoever it was didn't see all the unusual elements being thrown around earlier.

A guy in cargo shorts and a tank ran toward me. "Your girl, dude! That was fucked. Get in, and we'll follow. Did you call the cops?"

I was never more thankful for a good Samaritan. "My buddy is calling them. Thank you."

Dude pointed to a nice sports car.

Fuck, yes. This baby would be fast.

I threw myself into the passenger seat, and the dude tore out of the lot after Red Shirt's car. They had a good head start, but we could see them ahead.

As we left the parking lot, I spotted Peanut running in the direction of the house and thanked all the elements.

We could not lose our girl.

CHAPTER TWENTY-FIVE

RIVER

Glancing out the window at the pouring rain, I frowned. Were Zephyr and Rae still out there? Why wouldn't they come home?

I needed something to occupy my mind, so I headed for the kitchen and grabbed a pot. Filling it with water, I set it on the stove to boil. A little comfort pasta would go a long way tonight.

Except waiting for water to boil didn't occupy enough of my mind.

I should have gone with him when he followed Rae, but the two of us would have been far more noticeable. I wasn't entirely sure I agreed with Zephyr and Ash, either, about her not going alone. The first time she'd been taken, she'd been with people, her brother, and Pierson. I didn't think any of us would deter whoever was after her.

"For fuck's sake, River!" Ash rushed into the kitchen and snatched the pot off the stove. "How many times have we told you not to cook? At least, not without supervision!"

Frowning, I sniffed the air. Nothing smelled off. "I was just boiling water."

"I know, and what happened the last time you tried to do that?" he demanded.

I didn't like it being brought up. How the hell was I to know water could be burned? Okay, so the pot burned because the water all boiled away, but same thing, really. It was a one-off.

"Why are you even cooking?" he demanded. "You never cook."

He had a point there. I wasn't very good at cooking, and since both Ash and Tarin were pretty good in the kitchen, I didn't bother. "I needed to occupy my mind. Didn't work."

Ash's expression softened with understanding. "Worrying about Rae and Zephyr?"

I nodded. Where the hell were they? With all this rain, I would think they'd head home.

A pounding on the door made both Ash and I jump.

Footsteps thundered down the hall above us as we both headed for the front door.

The pounding started up again.

Tarin came bounding down the stairs. "Who the hell is that?"

"No idea," I answered.

Ash threw open the door to find a soaked, out of breath Pierson on our doorstep. He shoved inside, shaking his head. His eyes held a wild, panicked look in them that chilled me to the bone.

"What happened?" I demanded.

No way everything was okay with him looking like that.

"Rae, guy, car," he panted, trying to catch his breath as he talked.

"Slow down, man. You need to breathe." Ash clapped a hand on Pierson's shoulder, but Pierson didn't seem willing to calm down.

He shook his head. "No time. Rae. Taken."

Oh, fuck. Of course.

Opening the foyer closet, I grabbed my shoes and tossed Ash's and Tarin's in their direction.

"Zephyr following." Pierson drew in a deep breath. "I don't know how he could catch them on foot, but…" He shrugged.

I didn't think he'd followed on foot, but

hopefully, he'd get rid of any evidence of wrongdoing he might have before getting caught.

"Tarin, call Quin and Brax. Let's get the Lex on the line." We were going to rescue Rae, but I wasn't about to think we'd be able to handle this on our own.

The Lex needed to be in on this.

I pulled my own phone out and dialed Zephyr.

"I didn't do anything illegal."

I cracked a grin at Zephyr's first words upon answering his phone. "I don't think I believe you, but we'll get into that later. Where are you?"

Only the sounds of breathing and the faint strains of music came through the line for a few moments.

"Not too far from the park. I didn't pay attention to the street signs." A pause followed. "Fuck. Kinda industrial area, it looks like."

"Zephyr, I love you, but you're a pain in my ass, you know that?" Pulling my phone from my ear, I swiped around until I found what I was looking for. Tapping the app, I waited a few for it to do its thing, then…bingo. "Okay, I got your location."

The closing of a door came over the line before Zephyr spoke again. "Thanks, man." Given that the words were faded, I could only guess he was talking to someone else. "How the hell do you know where I am?"

This time I knew he spoke to me.

I grinned before I spoke. "You remember that app we played with for fun? The track your—"

"Oh, fuck you," Zephyr said without malice.

This time, I did laugh. "Love ya, boo. See ya soon. Don't lose sight of our girl."

I hung up on his sputtering. Damn, it was fun to tease him.

My smile dropped as I met the faces around me. "Okay, I got a location. Let's get going." We all filed out the door, but when Pier joined us, I held up a hand. "No. Not a good idea."

"She's my best friend. I'm not letting you guys go rescue her without me." He crossed his arms over his chest, but I still shook my head.

"Things might get hinky, and we aren't going it alone. We called... the right people, authorities," I told him. "Rae would never forgive us if something happened to you because we let you come along."

"But I can do things, apparently..." He started with conviction that trailed off into uncertainty.

With a wave of his hand, a few drops of rain gathered loosely, swept to the side, then dropped limply to the ground.

"Um, okay. We'll figure that out later, but it's even more reason for you to stay here. You're completely untrained, and that could be dangerous to us and Rae." I clamped a hand down on his shoulders as his face fell and his arms dropped. "I promise we'll call the second we have her safe."

Pierson nodded, then sank onto the steps.

I had a feeling he wouldn't be moving from that spot until we called him. I could only hope we wouldn't be leaving him waiting too long.

The three of us piled into my SUV, and I passed my phone off to Ash in the passenger seat. I knew where I was going, but if they moved or something happened, Zephyr would call us.

The hardest part was not speeding through the streets.

Who knew what our Raegan was going through? Was she being tortured? Mentally? Physically? What the hell did this person want with Raegan, anyway?

With my mind straying to dark places, I wanted to tear through town, storm this jerk's stronghold, and generally be a caveman. I was used to feeling protective. My mom and Bethany were my world, and I was all they had to shield them from those who'd take advantage of them. But this feeling was on an entirely different level, one I struggled to figure out.

As we neared the spot Zephyr's phone pinged, I slowed and searched for a parking spot. No need to pull right up and alert whatever guards there were.

I found one that put us out of sight but wasn't too far of a walk.

We locked up the car and headed for Zephyr. None of us spoke along the way, the same as on the drive over. Too much tension hung around us, and I figured Ash and Tarin were as lost in the dark places as I was.

When we finally approached our destination, I searched for Zephyr, not actually expecting him to be standing on the sidewalk or anything.

He stepped out of an alley and waved to us.

We followed him deeper into the shadows.

"Update?" I asked.

"Please tell me she's okay." Ash's voice shook.

I knew how he felt.

Zephyr shook his head. "I don't know. I haven't managed to lay eyes on her. All I know is the car went around the back side of that building and when my ride tried to follow, we found a fence around the back side. Car couldn't have gone out anywhere else from what I've seen."

Creeping to the edge of the alley, he pointed to a nondescript, beige, block building with a plain, glass front door and a small window to the side. It didn't look like much of a storefront or office building and held an air of abandonment.

Perfect for dickheads who kidnapped innocent girls.

Tarin peered around the corner like he knew what he was looking at. "Have you checked it out yet?"

The only one here who might have any idea of how to case a building, or sneak into one, was Zephyr. The rest of us didn't have any clue. But apparently, we were all determined to act like we were pros.

"Beyond driving around it, no," Zephyr said grimly. "I didn't see anyone hanging around outside. I don't think we'll have much issue getting in."

Whoever was behind all this didn't seem to be very good at being bad guys. Why would they leave their base of operations open like that? Or maybe I had been watching too many superhero movies with Mom lately.

I shook my head. "We're all idiots, but let's go get our girl. I don't want to wait for the Lex."

"They aren't far behind us." Tarin said. "I texted them the location as soon as we got in the car."

"Don't care if they come or not, I'm not waiting any longer." Zephyr rounded the corner, twisting his hands to gather air around them. The rest of us were barely two steps behind.

I pulled a small green flask with a cute wooden button decoration from my pocket. Finding water wasn't usually an issue since I found I could actually pull it from pipes half the time, but that wasn't reliable.

Instead, I prefer to carry the flask. It had the added bonus of functioning as a water bottle for me.

Ash pulled his lighter from his pocket while Tarin drew dirt up from the ground with a wave of his hand.

Nearing the building, I noticed it was concrete, which might present a problem.

Concrete buildings sometimes interfered with our abilities. No one knew why, or if they did, no one told the rest of us. As we neared, I kept waiting for an attack, for some guard or minion to jump out at us, but it never materialized.

Zephyr threw open the front door, I couldn't help but think this was too easy.

We rushed inside, only to be blinded by a sudden bright light and a high-pitched screech. Pinpricks of pain speared my chest, like tiny metal darts embedded themselves in my skin.

On instinct, I threw a hand out, but nothing happened. I blinked against the blindness from the light, stars dancing in my vision. My brain felt fuzzy. I wanted to check on the others, but it was all could I do to keep a straight thought in my head.

Rough hands grabbed me from behind, closing around my arms.

I fought the hold, or tried to, anyway. Too much fuzz in my head, and my limbs felt like limp noodles.

My arms were dragged behind me. Cold steel closed around them, and for a moment, I hoped they'd leave it at that. If I could still move my hands, I could still control my element.

That hope was dashed to pieces a moment later when those rough hands forced the palms of my hands together and began winding a rope around them.

I fought against it as best I could, but whatever they'd set off when we entered had messed us up good. I could hear Zephyr cursing and threatening. Tarin wasn't any better, though he wasn't cursing. He was resorting to name-calling.

Ash's silence bothered me the most. You never wanted him silent.

The men who held me tied the rope off just under the cuffs and finally let me go.

I rose to my toes, planning to spin and kick whoever tied my hands. Maybe I'd get lucky and knock him down or something.

Instead, a hard kick to the back of my knees sent me to the floor, and a hand clasped around my throat in threat.

Finally, the fog began to clear, and a figure emerged from a door on the far side of the room. "Well, that worked better than I thought."

CHAPTER TWENTY-SIX

RAEGAN

My captor wasn't making a lot of sense.

Of course, he wasn't really talking to me, either, more mumbling under his breath.

He'd contained me in some kind of force field. I'd spent more time trying to figure out what element it could be part of than trying to figure out a way to escape. Was it an aspect of air, some advanced form of the protective shield Zephyr could conjure?

Whatever it was, I knew I couldn't leave it. I'd tried that much, and my captor didn't need to concentrate to hold it.

"Joshua, answer me!" a person yelled from nearby.

I hadn't been able to get a visual on the speaker, but whoever they were, the voice failed to be distinctive enough to determine gender. They weren't happy with my captor, though. They'd been upset from the moment he set me down and enclosed me in this invisible cage.

"What the hell have you done?" the voice demanded. "Why did you bring her here?"

The man who'd captured me stood close by, but he faced away from me toward the other speaker. "I did what was—"

A loud blaring sound interrupted him.

He spun on his heel to look at me. "Stupid idiots came after you. This should prove interesting."

He dashed out of the room, leaving me to stew in my thoughts.

He'd been muttering about what he needed to do, what he'd been promised, the rise of the Enlightened one. It seemed like mad ramblings, but then he'd turn to me with this sappy smile on his face, eyes unfocused.

The only thing he'd said to me was, "You're finally home," in a voice not quite his own.

He hadn't even asked me for anything or to do anything. I kept waiting for the demands or for some clue about why he wanted me so badly, but it never came.

"Rae!" Ash's voice jerked my head around.

I hadn't really registered what Joshua had said when he left, but now, he led the way as four men clad head to toe in black—cliche much?—shoved the boys forward until they stood nearby.

"Ash! Why did you come after me?" The moment the words left my mouth, I felt like an idiot.

Of course, they'd come after me. I was part of their Genus, and they were a tad overprotective.

Ash just gave me a *duh* look before turning to our captor. "The Lex are on the way."

Joshua ignored him.

I couldn't let the boys suffer for me. I'd find a way out or figure something out. I didn't even know what this man wanted. Maybe it wouldn't be too bad. Optimistic probably, but a girl could hope.

"Joshua!" I called out. "Let them go. Please."

He spun in my direction, tilted his head, and scanned my body.

"They aren't of any concern to the Enlightened One, are they?" I held my breath, unsure if I'd gotten it right. "I'm the one the Enlightened One wants. They're just nobodies."

"Rae," the growl was a warning from Tarin that I ignored.

I'd do whatever it took to make sure they were

safe, then I'd get the fuck away from looney Joshua and whatever Enlightened One he worked for.

"You have a point, love." Joshua tilted his head in the boys' direction. "But even nobodies can be... persuaded to join us." He turned his attention back to me. "But you are right. The Enlightened One only needs you. They can be useful among my own men."

This was good, sort of. I needed him to let them go, though. Especially since it sounded like he might do something violent to them otherwise. I couldn't let that happen.

I threw a glance their way.

Every face held harsh lines, their hands twisted and tied behind them, the tension in their bodies revealing their discomfort. They wouldn't be happy with what I was about to do. As a matter of fact, they'd be downright pissed, but I was going to do it, anyway.

"I'll go with you," I spoke with desperation heavy in my voice and knew Joshua heard it. It could only help my cause. "Wherever it is you need me to go, or whoever I need to see. I'll go. Without a fight, no resistance. As long as you let them leave. Please. They're nothing to you."

The boys started screaming and hollering at me.

I tuned them out. This was the only way. Joshua's

defenses would be down, thinking I would be a willing participant, and that would give me an opening.

Hopefully.

Joshua's head jerked back to me. "Truly?" He stalked toward me, eyes narrowed. "How far would you go to let them be free?"

His words sent a shiver down my spine, like a snake.

Ick.

"The Enlightened One promised me to make my family whole again. To return my love to me." He stopped in front of my cage. "Will you not fight that? Hmm? Will you come willingly when ordered to do so?"

The hollering from the boys grew louder and more assertive, but I continued to tune it out. If I let myself listen, I might break down, or back out.

Keeping my eyes on Joshua, I nodded.

"Prove it." He waved a hand, and the force field imprisoning me disappeared.

The second the shimmer was gone, I wanted to run, but if I did that, I would put the boys in more danger. Joshua already showed he wasn't above using them to get me to cooperate.

He stepped forward, bringing himself into my space, then lifted a hand to my cheek.

Everything in my body screamed to rebel, to kick him in the nuts or shove him or something. I didn't do any of it. Instead, I leaned into the touch with a small smile, forced though it was. I couldn't help the tension in my body that mirrored the boys, but I hadn't told him I'd like it.

His thumb ran over my cheek as he leaned in and pressed a kiss to the corner of my mouth.

I forced myself not to jerk back, to simply stand there and accept it.

As he withdrew, he laughed. "Oh, this will be delicious. Yes, yes. I think this will be fine." He waved a hand at the boys. "Release them, then see them off the property. If they deign to come back after their lives have been so prettily bargained for, kill them."

"No!" I failed to stop the shout from slipping out. When Joshua frowned, I took a deep breath and spoke more calmly. "That wasn't part of the deal."

Joshua merely shook his head. "You said let them go, not let them live, my dear. If they're foolish enough to come charging right back in..." He shrugged as though that said it all.

He waved a hand again in their direction, and this time, his minions moved to undo the boys' bindings.

He must have tied their hands somehow if they'd been unable to use their power. Joshua grabbed my arm and pulled me toward the far end of the room.

The direction he led me only had a blank wall was at that end. As I stared, wondering where we were going, a swirl of color appeared on the wall, like something out of a fantasy.

What kind of Elementum could do that?

My eyes darted back to the boys. By the looks on their faces, they wouldn't go quietly.

"Just leave!" I hollered at them as tears streamed down my face. "Don't worry about me. I'll be fine. You need to let me go! Please!"

Ash shook his head, mouth a thin line. His hands were fisted at his sides, a slight movement catching my eyes. A glint of light told me he held his lighter.

No, no, no. They needed to go, or Joshua would kill them. Those minions of his were too close. "Please, just forget me, okay? I caused nothing but problems!"

Ash wasn't the only one with his hands fisted or power ready.

Dammit! Why weren't they listening?

"You boys better listen to her before I renege on our deal," Joshua sneered at them. "She's where she belongs now, which was never with you four."

I threw my hand up, thrusting everything inside me out at once, all the feelings and emotions. The fear, the determination, everything, hoping they'd feel it as well and know I had a plan.

"Just go!" I screamed for all I was worth.

Something shimmered through the air as the boys each let loose their own power.

Suddenly, the elements whirled together like a hurricane of nature. With no idea what was happening, I continued to feed everything inside me toward them. On the edge of my awareness, the sound of shouting reached me, accompanied by pounding feet.

Then, the world exploded with light as a door burst open.

The nature hurricane compacted, the elements creating a snug little ball. Earth mixed into water, water mixed into fire and air swirled around the whole thing. I watched as first mud formed, then air dried, then fire hardened and heated. The whole thing took seconds but felt like time suspended itself, then sped back up as the whole thing exploded with pure force.

More shouts filled the air as Joshua's minions hit the ground, the force of nature knocking them out cold.

As the familiar badges of the Lex appeared around us, the firm grip on my arm released itself. I didn't bother questioning or waiting. I simply ran straight to the boys.

They engulfed me quickly, then stepped back. I took the moment to look around and realized utter chaos had descended. People were everywhere, both the lex and the minions who hadn't been surrounding the guys. Smoke filled the air, and shouting accompanied it, panic taking over the minions.

And then, I realized I didn't see Joshua.

"Where is he?" I shouted above the chaos and panic, my head swiveling around, desperately seeking the one person who should be taken in above everyone else.

"Who?" River shouted in my ear.

"Joshua! The guy who took me!" I searched more frantically. "I don't see him!"

All the boys searched the room, but it became obvious that none of us could find him.

"There!" Zephyr pointed toward the wall where the swirl of color appeared before.

It had vanished in the chaos, but now, it reappeared. Joshua stood in front of it. He lifted his head, looked over his shoulder, and met my eyes.

The grin that slid over his face held possession

and malice. He said something. We were too far away to hear, and I couldn't read lips.

When he winked, I figured it had likely been something along the lines of watching me or catching up with me later, or something else creepy in a similar vein. As his gaze raked my body, it felt like a million tiny insects crawled over my skin.

Then, a swarm of Lex blocked my view.

At least, I thought they were Lex. It became hard to tell, the room a mass of bodies and chaos.

The boys steered me to the door, and I went willingly. I wanted out of here, away from everything. My body wanted to stop, my brain already shut down.

A sob escaped as everything that happened finally overwhelmed me.

We barely made it out the door when I finally collapsed.

CHAPTER TWENTY-SEVEN

ASH

O ur girl crumpled the second we walked out the door of the building.

None of us expected it, but we probably should have. Thankfully, Zephyr stood right behind her and scooped her up before she hit the sidewalk.

When River made to take her from him, he shook his head and pulled her closer. Maybe he was finally warming up to her.

"She all right?" Tarin moved close and pressed his hand to her forehead.

I couldn't help but roll my eyes. She wasn't sick, for Element's sake.

He let his hand fall away, then turned to me. "Let's get home."

He jerked his head to the side, and I could read the message he sent. Too many years as best friends came in handy sometimes.

I turned toward home and walked a bit ahead of River, Zephyr, and Rae.

Tarin caught me in no time. "We should talk."

I nodded, knowing exactly what he wanted to talk about. Our relationship had been weird since Rae came to us. I hadn't made my interest in Rae a secret at all, and Tarin, well, I couldn't quite figure out how interested he actually was.

I said nothing, letting him gather his thoughts.

"I've been poking at you since Rae came," he said. "I'm sorry about that."

I'd suspected as much, at least at first. Rae was the first girl in a long time that I'd been truly interested in, not just lusting for. When it was sex, well, sex was easy. Actual interest in a girl made me freeze and feel awkward.

"Was that all it was?" I asked.

"At first, yeah." Tarin shook his head. "I wanted to spark you to actually make a move."

"I was already making a move," I grumbled. "We were going for walks at night, and I kissed her way before you did."

He winced. "Again, I'm sorry. I thought you were

still hesitating. And then, I spent some time with Rae and, man…" He breathed the last word on a sigh.

Fuck, I knew exactly what he meant.

"Yep. She's something else. So much, just right under the surface, waiting to burst out." I glared at him. "I was pissed at first that you made a move on her knowing I liked her. It hurt, especially when it didn't feel genuine. But if you honestly have feelings for her, you have to know I won't have an issue with you being with her, too. I mean, look at our world. Look at my sister." I stopped walking and turned toward him. "But it's not a competition. You know that, right?"

"I know. I just…" He shrugged again.

I'd never known Tarin to struggle with expressing himself. Weird.

"Didn't all your sister's guys kind of fall at once?" he asked hesitatingly. "I like Rae. She's pretty awesome, and there's for sure something there, but you already seem half in love with her."

I couldn't help laughing. We'd both grown up around all of this and here Tarin was acting as green as the leaves he loved. "Dude, what is with you? You know that's not how it works. We're still individuals."

With a shake of his head, Tarin laughed, too. "You're right. I've been stupid."

"Hey! You two going to flap your traps all day or are you getting in the damn car?" Zephyr hollered, making both of us start.

I spun, heat flaring under my skin that I fought back. I'd totally forgotten where we were. No idea what Tarin's excuse was.

We both jogged over to the SUV. River was already behind the wheel, so I headed for the back passenger door while Tarin ran around to the other side. As I climbed into the back seat, and Tarin slid in from the opposite side, I stared at the empty spot between us in confusion before peering into the front.

Zephyr still held Rae, who'd snuggled against his chest in the front passenger seat.

"You can't hold her on your lap for the trip home." I reached between the seats to finagle her into the back with us, but the glare Zephyr shot at me made me think twice.

Turned out I didn't need to worry, because right then, Rae's eyes fluttered.

She rubbed her face against Zephyr, then seemed to realize where she was. "I... I...I'm sorry."

Cheeks red, she tried to scramble off him, but there wasn't anywhere to go.

"You're fine, troublemaker. But now that you're

awake, you should probably climb in back with the others." Zephyr nodded in our direction.

Since we hadn't taken off yet, she climbed out of the front and crawled between me and Tarin in the back.

I wrapped an arm around her shoulders and noticed Tarin tangle their hands together.

The trip home was quiet. I didn't know about the others, but my mind kept drifting back to the end, to the sudden explosion, for lack of better words.

What the hell had happened?

Not wanting to disrupt or worry Rae needlessly, I pulled my phone from my pocket and shot off a text.

Ash: Hey, have Mammy meet us at the house.

A ding came from Tarin's phone, and he cut me a glance before pulling it from his pocket to respond.

Tarin: Not a bad idea. Thinking about that elemental hurricane, too?

Looking over Rae's head, I met his eyes and nodded.

Leaving Tarin to text to Mammy, I squeezed Rae's shoulders. "You okay?"

Her pale eyes drifted up to meet mine. "I... I don't know." She frowned, adorable little wrinkles creasing her forehead. "Physically, I'm fine. He didn't really hurt me, but..."

"There's a lot more to being okay than physical." I pressed a kiss to the top of her head as we pulled into the driveway at the house.

As if he'd been standing at the door, which he might well have been, Pierson flew out as River killed the engine. Since getting trampled wasn't high on my list today, I exited the car fast and left the door open for Rae to follow.

She'd barely stepped out when Pierson engulfed her in a tight hug.

She fell against him, muttering. Figuring she was reassuring him, I left them to their moment.

Tarin, on the other hand, glared at him.

I stopped beside him, laid a hand on his shoulder, and whispered in his ear, "Dude's gay, man."

It had only taken seeing him around Rae's brother for me to figure that one out.

Tarin actually started and looked at me, questions in his eyes.

"Okay, so I'm guessing at that." Tarin dead-stared me, but I kept going, "But he's for sure not into our girl. He's crushing hard on her brother."

He spun, and we both headed inside, but not before he glanced back to Rae and Pierson. "How do you know that?"

I snorted. "Pay attention to the way he looks at Devin. You'll get it."

Knowing how hard the adrenaline crash was going to be, I headed for the kitchen and grabbed several electrolyte drinks from the fridge.

By the time I made it to the living room, everyone had taken seats with Rae sprawled on the floor.

I passed the drinks around as the front door opened and Mammy strode in. "Well, what have my favorite troublemakers gotten up to now?" Her gaze found Rae, and she frowned. "You look like a wet chihuahua, honey." She sank down beside Rae and wrapped an arm around her. "Now, you all just tell Mammy what's happened."

Not up to rehashing it, I let River and Zephyr fill her in. Tarin occasionally piped up, too.

I'd taken a seat in a chair close to Rae and slid my foot, so it just rested against her. She looked back over her shoulder with a tired smile for me before returning her attention to Mammy.

When they finished, Mammy frowned with concern. "Well, now, that's quite a tale. I wonder if this is at all related to what happened with Sera?"

That drew my attention, and I sat up straighter. "No. No way." I shook my head rapidly. "Chester is dead. He blew the fuck up in that car. And he was a nut job, anyway."

The idea of my sister still being in danger from the freak who'd stalked her a year ago terrified me. Forget what it did when I added the girl I was falling for into that mix.

"We never did figure out why he wanted your sister so badly. Maybe he wasn't alone."

Elements! That made too much sense for my comfort.

"Wait." Rae peered at me. "Sera? What happened to her? What are you talking about?"

"A year ago, Sera was being stalked by this nut job named Chester. He kept trying to convince her she belonged with him because she's a Prime, a direct descendant of the original four blessed by the Mother. But he died in a car explosion." I turned my gaze to Mammy. "He. Died," I said firmly, slowly, needing to emphasize the words.

"Well, we won't solve that tonight." Mammy didn't sound as convinced as I wanted her to be before she tuned back to Rae. "Let's talk about what happened with your powers. Describe it to me again."

With everyone pitching in, we went over what happened one more time in detail.

Mammy asked several questions, but her gaze kept returning to Rae.

Finally, she held up a hand to stop us. "Rae, just before the element whirlwind, what did you do?"

Rae stilled before her pale eyes widened. "I, uh, I was…" She frowned as she stumbled over her words. "I was upset and trying to get the boys to leave. Something swelled up inside me, just like all this emotion I guess, and I yelled at them to leave."

"Hmm. Did you make any movements?" Mammy pressed. "Do anything with the feeling inside you?"

"Oh, uh, yeah. I threw a hand up. And all the emotion just felt like too much, so I kind of…thrust it out?" Her voice rose at the end, making it a question.

I couldn't handle watching her seem so uncertain anymore, so I rose and crossed to where she sat. When she looked up at me with a frown, I pulled her up and into my arms, hugging her tight, then sat where she'd just been and pulled her into my lap.

For a moment, she was stiff before she relaxed into my embrace.

"I thought so." Mammy shifted in her seat before continuing. "I believe you inadvertently tried to combine their powers."

"What?"

"That's not possible."

"No way."

"Impossible."

We all spoke at once, but Rae looked thoughtfully at Mammy. "Can't they do that, anyway?"

Mammy shook her head. "No. Every element is unique and separate. We only control the purest form of the element."

"So, if you tried to put water and fire together..." Rae nibbled her bottom lip.

Mammy nodded and smiled. "You'd get a doused fire."

I planted a kiss on Rae's forehead. Leave it to my girl to get it right away.

"Now, obviously, you didn't even know you could do this, so all you did was get the elements to swirl around together," Mammy continued. "With more training, you could combine elements to create other things. Mist, for example."

Wow, that could be incredibly useful.

Rae sank further against me, and I leaned forward to peer at her. Her eyes drooped, and one hand reached up to clutch at my shirt.

When I looked up, I met River's eyes.

He came over and lifted Rae out of my lap.

"She's wiped," River spoke softly, but Rae barely stirred.

She wasn't asleep, but it was a near thing.

"Yes, I can see that." Mammy rose and gathered her purse. "You boys take special care of her. She's going to need you all, I think, before any of this is done."

She strode out the door with River carrying Rae behind her. He gently kicked the front door closed, then headed upstairs with Rae.

I met Tarin and Zephyr's gazes, and saw my own worries reflected in them. "She's right, you know. I think this is only just beginning."

Neither of them responded, but they didn't need to. They'd been there as my best support when I'd struggled to accept the sister I didn't know I had, when that same sister had been stalked, and for the aftermath of her abduction, short though it was.

So now, when the person in danger was much, much closer to all of us, they were right here in the flames with me.

River rejoined us and leaned against the doorjamb. He didn't speak, either, for several minutes.

When he finally spoke, he said the words we were all thinking. "Nothing is going to happen to her. Not while I breathe."

I didn't know what crazy had come into my life now, but I knew we'd do anything to keep it as far away from our Spirit as we could.

To Be Continued

CLAIMING FLAME
ELEMENTUM GENUS BOOK 1

Labeled a misfit, Sera's stopped trying to fit in as she bounced from one boarding school to the next. When three determined guys take an active interest in her, can she keep them at a distance?

After years of being shuttled from school to school, Sera has built walls to keep others out, too afraid of being hurt when she has to leave. So, when Souta, JJ, and Brooks, all part of the same Genus, take an interest in her, she tries to keep them at arm's length just like everyone else.

But being without friends comes at a risk. Sera's never been one to keep her opinions to herself, and she draws the wrath of the dorm matron, Aguirre, who knows just how to keep young Elementums in their place.

Will Sera accept the friendship and mystical connection Souta, JJ, and Brooks offer, and the possible protection that comes with it? Or will Aguirre's rage and need for control destroy her? As an important date for Sera looms closer, can she learn that her real strength, confidence, and courage lie in letting these men in?

ABOUT THE AUTHOR

Desi Lin first put paper to pen after her fourth-grade teacher encouraged her to explore her natural talent. Already a lover of books and the infinite worlds and possibilities they brought with them, it took little for her to begin to create her own stories. A writer was born. She continued to use her writing as an escape from a world she struggled with until some incredible birds took her under their wing and nurtured her from writer to full-blown author. Now she spends her day arguing with the voices inside her head, playing taxi for her four kids, or attempting to make her home look a little less like a hurricane destroyed it. She lives in Central Florida where she can be found listening to music, dancing around her living room, creating art, or playing D&D when not writing.

Made in the USA
Columbia, SC
23 January 2023